Whiskey River Rescue

Whiskey River Rescue

A Whiskey River Romance

Justine Davis

TULE
PUBLISHING

Dedication

For Pretty Face, who taught me the hard way
never to fall for a pretty face.

For Sassafras, sweet Sassy, and
sunset rides on the beach.

And for The Black, Inky, Sham, Misty, Flicka, Brego,
Shadowfax, and all the fictional horses
who have lived in my mind and heart.

And even—or especially—for the Thestrals.

Acknowledgments

To my friends and great writers Eve Gaddy and Kathy Garbera: thanks for letting me play in Booze's fountain!

Chapter One

IT WAS A beautiful day, Kelsey Blaine thought, considering the world had just turned upside down on her. It should be snowing, unlikely as that was in the Texas Hill Country, because she felt like she was in a snow globe, getting shaken by hands she had no control over.

"I'm sorry, Kelsey. I hate to see the land go, but it's just the way things are. I couldn't afford to turn down an offer like that. It's going to solve all my major money problems, and let me hire some help around the house."

She gave herself an inward shake. Her problems were minor, compared to Jim Roper's. The crusty old man was fighting to save his home. She shouldn't begrudge him this windfall just because it happened to impact her. He'd already been more than generous, for a long time.

She'd land on her feet, somehow. Besides, it wasn't herself she was really worried about. It was the horses. "I understand, Jim. Really."

"I still can't believe anyone was willing to pay that much for only twenty-five acres," Jim said.

"It is. . . unexpected," she said. Then, with sudden concern for the kind man, she asked, "You're sure it's legit?"

Jim smiled. "Oh, I had my doubts. Thought somebody was trying to scam an old man. But Megan Clark handled it, and you know no one puts anything over on her. She said the money—in cash, if you can believe it—was already in an escrow account before the offer was even made."

The local real estate agent was indeed a sharp, smart woman, and Kelsey felt better. She took a gulp of the coffee that had become just cool enough to swallow quickly. She needed the jolt. Not that the news the land she and the Whiskey River Rescue horses been living on had just been sold out from under them wasn't enough jolt for this Monday morning.

"I should have told you sooner, but—"

"You were ill," she said, waving off the apology. She knew trying to keep up the family place was wearing on the older man more and more, and he'd just spent two weeks in the hospital, only getting out yesterday. Pressure from her was the last thing he needed, so she changed the subject. "So, who is this person who apparently has money to spare?"

"Well, now," Jim said, taking a sip of his own dark brew, "that's the funny part. Don't know."

Kelsey blinked. "What?"

"It's all being handled by some lawyer out of Dallas, for something called the Shipley Trust."

"A trust?"

"Megan says it's all under a demand of confidentiality," Jim said. "Otherwise the deal's off."

"Secretive sort?"

"Maybe just private." Jim grinned at her. "Some folks don't believe in plastering their lives all over the interwebs, y'know."

Kelsey laughed. Jim might be older, but he was one of the most tech savvy people she knew. If he'd been charging the locals for all the tech repair work and consulting advice he'd given over the years, he could be buying more land, not selling it.

"I really am sorry, Kelsey. I know this was a shock, but you'll be fine, it'll end up being better, I'm sure—"

She stopped him, laying her hand comfortingly over his. "Thank you, but don't say another word. And don't you worry. You've got enough to deal with. I'll be—"

She heard the door of the coffee shop open, and interrupted her reassurances to Jim when she saw his fishing buddies, men she knew only as the two Georges, approaching. She patted his hand once more and, after some teasing from them about Jim's secret lunch with a pretty girl, left them to discussing the one that got away, or whatever it was they talked about.

As she left, she wished she felt as confident as she'd sounded. She'd wanted to reassure Jim, and she had—but in truth she had no idea what she was going to do. Finding enough space for the six horses she currently had for anything close to the pittance Jim had charged them for three of those twenty-five acres, let alone with a place for her to live, was going to be next to, if not on the other side of, impossible.

She thought of Cocoa, the sweet-natured little chocolate palomino who had been barely able to move when Kelsey had pulled her out of that collapsed barn, and who had been written off as a loss by an owner ready to send her to slaughter. And Mac, the sleek bay quarter horse who had been headed the same direction, despite his one-time potential as a show horse, when he'd gone blind. Then her beautiful Granite, who'd had the misfortune to be bought by a couple from some big Eastern city, who knew nothing of horses and had merely wanted essentially a lawn ornament to complete the picture they had in their minds of what a "gentleman's ranchette" looked like.

And the others, all variations on a theme, animals who had been abandoned or neglected or even abused by the humans who were responsible for them. It moved her as nothing else did, and had brought her to this pass.

She walked down the street, trying to think of what to do. She paused in front of the book store, as if the answer could be found in some tome of wisdom displayed in the window. But the only thing there was a large arrangement, complete with character cutouts and artwork from local young fans, of the latest Sam Smith mega-best seller. Nothing that would be of any help to her, although loosing herself in a good book, even a children's book, sounded immensely appealing right now. Maybe especially a children's book.

"Kelsey! What are you going to do?"

Kelsey turned to see Teri Crane, who worked in the office at the church on the corner, watching her anxiously. News had obviously travelled fast, but then it always did in Whiskey River. "Not sure yet."

"But how can he do that, sell the land right out from under you?"

"It's getting harder for him to keep up with that big house, plus he was sick and got behind. He needed the money and doesn't have much choice."

"But it's still awful."

Kelsey shook her head. "He's let us stay on that piece of land for next to nothing for three years now. It's not his fault if he can't afford it anymore."

"Well, when you put it that way," the petite blonde said, sounding chastened.

That was the good thing about Teri. She leapt to the defense of her friends, but she saw reason, too. Sometimes it had to be pointed it out to her, but if it was there, she eventually saw it.

Kelsey walked to Dr. Barrett's office. Since he was a big animal vet his work was done in the field, but he had this small office in town for paperwork and for people to pick up necessities and prescriptions, which was what she was here for.

When she walked into the reception area, the tall brunette behind the counter waved at Kelsey as she continued to speak into the phone she held. Multitasking was a skill Edie Mays had mastered. Kelsey had seen her check in one patient while inputting the billing data for another, while printing and stapling receipts for yet another checking out, all the while maintaining a coherent conversation with someone else on the phone.

"If you could bottle that, I'd buy it by the gallon," she'd once told her.

"Why I make the really big bucks," Edie had said with a laugh.

Kelsey had laughed, too. Big bucks weren't why she— and most others, she thought—lived in Whiskey River. It was the people and the quality of life here. And the history, if you were into that.

"Guess this puts your youth camp on hold," Edie said now, confirming that the news had reached her as well.

"So much for big plans." Kelsey said it lightly, but that one hurt.

She'd been so fired up about starting her horse camp this summer, bringing together horses and kids who had seen the worst side of human nature, but she couldn't very well do that when her horses were about to become homeless. And thinking about that side of human nature always sparked her temper. This was Texas, for God's sake. They should have more respect for the animal that was so much a part of its history. As much as for the longhorn that was represented everywhere, at least.

She almost laughed at her own snit, and was over it by the time Edie finished her phone call.

The woman reached beneath the counter and handed her a white paper bag that was surprisingly heavy; the tube of salve for Mac's fetlock gash must be a big one.

"Oh, the lady from the county shelter was in earlier," Edie said. "They'll probably be calling you for some photos on some new arrivals. Puppies."

Kelsey let out a breath. Taking funny or appealing photos of shelter pets, which had proven countless times to be the key to quick adoptions, was another of her passions, although at the moment it wasn't at the top of her list. She'd have to explain when they called that she had a big problem to solve first. Although puppies weren't a hard sell, when photographed right. She'd find the time, somehow. After all, it was that work that had led her to founding the Whiskey River Rescue, when she'd realized there were far fewer rescues who could handle horses.

"So, did you find out who's buying the property out from under you?" Edie asked.

"No," Kelsey said. "It's all hush-hush. Some trust or something."

"You should find out who's behind it. Maybe they'll let you stay."

"Why would someone buy it unless they had plans for

it?"

"I guess," Edie said. "But you could ask. You don't ask, you don't get, my grandma used to say."

Kelsey laughed, asked Edie to give her thanks to Dr. Barrett, who more often than not donated his care and medicine, and headed off to the feed store to do her monthly song and dance. She hated it, hated having to coax, cajole, even beg help from those who could provide what the horses needed. It was against her self-sufficient nature, but for the horses who counted on her, she would do things she would normally never do.

She'd just convinced Sack's Supply to throw in two extra bags of sweet feed—the stuff did have a shelf-life, after all, and those bags were getting close—when her cell phone rang. She'd been able to prepay it this month, although it was a bare bones plan. She'd gotten rather good at stretching her limited income. The small inheritance from her father was her mainstay, and she supplemented that with her work as a freelance photographer, although she donated those services to the animal shelters and other rescues who called. But the horse rescue expenses were high, and were it not for that large donation a couple of months ago both the cell phone and the feed troughs would be empty.

"Kelsey?"

"Hi, Edie," she said, recognizing the voice. "Did I forget something?"

"No, no," the woman assured her. "Look, Mrs. Murray

was just in, to pick up her cat. Remember, she works at the county offices?"

"Yes," Kelsey said, placing the woman she'd always thought a bit of a busybody in her mind.

"You know how she gossips," Edie said. "Well, she just told me who's behind the trust that bought the land. You won't believe it."

Although she wasn't sure what good it would do her to know, Kelsey asked anyway, because Edie was a friend and was clearly trying to be helpful. "Who?"

"Crazy Joe."

Kelsey blinked. She hadn't expected *that.* "Kilcoyne?"

"Do we have another Crazy Joe?"

She didn't like the nickname, but she had to admit, no, they didn't. For a town the size of Whiskey River they had their share of people who might count as . . . eccentric. But Joseph Kilcoyne was the only one who'd earned the appellation of crazy. Mainly because he'd not only bought the old castle, but moved in from wherever he came from, and was never seen or heard from again. If it weren't for the various deliveries made, and the few workers coming and going, they'd never know he was even still alive out there, holed up in that big, odd place that sat in the middle of nearly a hundred acres, all alone.

"It makes sense, I guess," Kelsey said. "It does border his property."

"Maybe he needs more room to bury the bodies," Edie

said in a mockingly creepy voice.

Kelsey laughed. She knew that was one end of the speculation about their mysterious resident, born of a play on his last name. The other end held him to be some kind of reclusive celebrity going under a fake name.

She, on the other hand, thought he might just be someone who didn't care for the world and chose to not be part of it. She wasn't sure she could blame him for that.

And he could, apparently, afford it. Having everything delivered definitely upped the outgo. She knew that too well, having to often balance the delivery charges on something against the gas money to go get it herself.

"Thanks, Edie. I think," she added before she ended the call.

She wasn't at all sure where this left her. Knowing who had bought the land her rescue was now on didn't make much difference. It was odd, though, that she hadn't even been approached about it. Jim had told her he didn't know what the new buyer's intentions were. Perhaps his hundred acres outside of town weren't enough, and he needed that twenty-five more. Including the three her place was on.

Once the bags of feed and a half-dozen bales of first-cutting alfalfa hay were secured in the back of her truck, she headed home. It wasn't much, the little two room cabin, it creaked in the slightest wind and the last spring rain had shown the leak in the roof had worsened, but she'd made it as comfortable as she could.

And she loved the front porch, where she could sit and look out over the Texas Hill Country she loved. She wondered how much longer she would have there. He had to give her notice, didn't he? He couldn't just throw her out. But no matter how much time it was, it wouldn't be enough.

She sighed as she made the turn onto the dirt road that lead to her place. She had no answers and, right now, no hope of any. She needed to think, long and hard. Maybe she'd saddle up Granite and ride down to the river this afternoon. Or forget the saddle, and let the big, gray get good and wet in the river he seemed to love as much as she did. He'd even gotten used to the inner tubers floating by, and they in turn usually grinned and waved at the horse and rider as the leisurely current carried them past in their large, floating donuts.

It always helped her think, to get out and away on a horse—

She slammed on the brakes. Stared past the corrals to where she usually parked.

There were at least five men and two vehicles here.

And a bulldozer.

They were mowing her house down.

Chapter Two

S HE KICKED UP some dirt when her truck skidded to a stop, but she didn't care. She jumped out and crossed the fifteen feet to the nearest guy at a run.

"What are you doing?"

It came out screechy, but she was a little panicked. The man she'd accosted jerked a thumb over his shoulder. "Talk to the boss. Blue shirt."

She saw the man standing by the corral fence, looking at Mac's bandaged leg. The leg she should be attending to right now, not dealing with this.

"What are you doing?" she repeated as she came to a halt in front of the man who looked vaguely familiar. Whether it was because she'd seen him before or because he reminded her of her of someone, she wasn't sure.

"You're the horse rescue lady?" he asked.

He sounded polite enough, but she ignored the question and repeated her own for the third time. "What are you doing?"

"Just getting started. The boss, the buyer—"

"Is not wasting any time, obviously! I only found out today the sale was final."

The man frowned. "It was final three weeks ago."

"And my landlord was in the hospital."

"Oh." The man sounded suitably chagrinned. "Well, we're here to—"

"I can see what you're here to do," she said, looking toward the cabin and seeing wood torn off the sides and shingles from the roof scattered around. "If I'd been here, would you have just started to tear it down around my head? Bulldoze it with me still inside?"

"Look, Miss. . . Blaine, isn't it?"

Only then did she notice the boxes sitting beside the truck. Boxes full of things that were very familiar. And some that were very intimate. Heat shot to her face as her gaze shot back to the man's face.

"Did y'all enjoy fondling my underwear?"

He had the grace to look embarrassed, at least. "We had Will pack it up. He's married, got little girls."

"And of course no pervert has ever been married or had children."

"Hey, now, Will's a good, solid guy, he'd never even think like that."

She forced herself to get off the path her angry accusation had sent them veering down, driven in part by the embarrassing knowledge that some of that underwear was old and worn because every dime went to the horses. Besides, she doubted she'd get much out of this guy. He was just doing a job he was apparently hired to do.

Destroy her home, such as it was.

"Never mind," she snapped. She'd deal with this herself.

"Look, there's going to be—"

"Don't even *talk* to me. I'm going straight to your boss."

The man looked startled, then amused. "Good luck with that."

The amusement really set her off. She turned on her booted heel and took a step back toward her truck. Then she stopped, looked back at the boxes containing her belongings. She dug angrily through them until she found her camera bag, the old, falling apart scrapbook full of the precious pictures she'd taken of her father, and the framed photo of herself astride Sassafras, her childhood Pony of the Americas. She grabbed the three items that she would entrust to no one else, and left at a run without a backward glance.

She climbed into her truck and left with a spin of tires and a spray of dirt and gravel that she hoped would reach the shiny, new SUV parked blocking her drive.

She had never been up to the house at Crazy Joe's. She'd heard about what locals called the castle, though, the big, rambling stone house that had been added to over the years until it was a mishmash of styles Megan had found difficult to sell.

She should have guessed before Edie had called, Kelsey thought as she tried to calm down. It was too much to think that, in little Whiskey River, Megan had had two such secretive clients, Crazy Joe and the buyer of Jim's land, so close together.

The gate across the long, curving drive was locked. Who did that, in Whiskey River?

Somebody paranoid that was who. She sat in her truck, still fuming. She was contemplating backing up to barrel right on through, calculating the extent of her anger against the likely cost of replacing the solid metal gate, when another option occurred to her. She did back up then, but only far enough to take the turn onto the barely visible track that ran along the back of Jim's land, up against the fence of Crazy Joe's ranch. Eventually she came to what she'd remembered, the spot in the fence where an old, no longer used gate had been wired closed. She'd come across it on one of the long walks to get Cocoa functional again.

Barely three minutes later, she was putting her wire clippers away in the truck's toolbox and climbing back in the driver's seat. She drove through the newly reopened gate at a slower pace than her mood wanted, because she wasn't sure what shape the old track—it was hardly distinct enough to be called a road—was in. She paused on the other side and went back to close the gate. She didn't know if Crazy Joe had any livestock about, but she didn't want to be responsible for any getting loose if he did.

She got back in the truck and followed the track. She had the fleeting thought she had no idea if it would actually lead her to the house, and that it could just as easily meander over the entire place, or dead end at the river. She'd have to keep her eyes open and if she spotted the house just head for it, road, trail, or track or not. That was what four-wheel drives were for, after all.

In the end, the house was easy enough to find. It sat in a lush, green oasis amid the browner surroundings. And Megan's description had been an understatement. One end of the stone house was a low, rambling ranch-style, while the other end, facing toward a bluff that looked out over the river, looked for all the world like a castle turret, like a hulking, ancient keep from some old Celtic tale.

This was what she could see from her place, the tall, rounded stone thing she'd thought was just a lookout over the river someone had built. But now, seeing it was part of the house itself, she found herself smiling at the whimsy of it despite her sour mood.

Something moved behind one of the tall, narrow windows in the round tower. She couldn't be sure what; it was at least three stories up. Her mouth quirked as she thought of slits in castle walls for archers and arrows, although these held glass. But she didn't forget why she was here. She parked the truck as close as she could get to what she guessed was the front door and, with a determined stride, headed that way.

There was no doorbell. At least, nothing she could see that resembled a button for one. The door was heavy looking, and when she tapped on it—she'd start out calmly, she ordered herself—the sound was so faint she thought the thing must be six inches thick.

When no one came she rapped harder, but still wasn't sure anyone inside could hear it. But somebody must have seen her drive up, the person in the tower if no one else. When a minute passed, she tried again, this time knocking hard enough that her knuckles protested.

Again she waited. Nothing. Mentally she calculated the time it would take to get from that upper tower to this door, if whoever had been up there happened to be the only person here. It didn't seem likely, a place this size, but all the town gossip indicated the man lived alone, and brought in household help from out of town. Apparently he didn't trust the locals not to talk—and, she admitted ruefully, with good reason, Whiskey River was like many small towns, its grapevine quick, thorough, and sometimes even accurate—and it was even rumored that his help all had to sign non-disclosure agreements, to never tell anyone anything about anything.

Which, she suspected, had given rise to the serial killer branch of speculation about Crazy Joe Kilcoyne.

This time, she hammered the door with the side of her fist as hard as she could and as long as she could, until her hand protested vigorously. And waited. Still nothing. The person in the tower could have made it here on hands and knees by now, she thought.

It occurred to her then that perhaps she had been seen when she pulled up. Seen and recognized, as the person having her home unceremoniously torn down practically around her ears.

Maybe Kilcoyne or one of his henchmen was purposely not answering the door, because they didn't want to deal with her.

"Stuff that," she muttered.

For a moment, she stood there, thinking. Nothing happened to disturb her train of thought; if Crazy Joe wanted peace and quiet, he certainly had it here. She walked down off the porch and started around the house. Maybe there was somebody outside, a workman or something. It certainly seemed like there should be at least a gardener, since keeping this landscaping in this shape was no easy task.

The place was even bigger than she'd thought, if she included the large garden she found out back, which included several mature pecan trees and a long narrow pool. For swimming laps? There was a covered patio that ran about half the length of the house, but still no sign of anyone.

An uneasy feeling came over her. She was, after all, in essence, trespassing. She might have a good reason to be here, but still. . .

Her burst of fury was fading fast. She never had been any good at maintaining anger for long. Mom had always said, "Anger made your mouth work faster than your mind, which almost always led to regret." And her mother was the wisest person Kelsey knew.

"Thirty point zero five."

Kelsey whirled, her breath stopping short in her throat.

A man stood less than six feet away. Tall, lean to the point of thinness, with dark hair, clean but a bit shaggy on top and mussed. Attractive, in a distinct kind of way. She couldn't guess at his age; his face appeared not much older than her, but his eyes were anciently weary. His long-sleeved t-shirt was faded, and where he had his left hand jammed into a pocket the cuff was unraveling. The jeans weren't in much better shape with a rip at one knee and seriously fraying at the hems. And in the other pocket she could see the handles of what looked like a small pair of garden clippers.

His expression was unreadable, as were his eyes, which were, she realized, a chilly sort of gray, fringed with dark, thick lashes.

"I—"

He cut her off, but in a casual tone. "That is the Texas Penal Code section for trespassing."

Uh-oh. Now she'd done it.

Chapter Three

"I WAS LOOKING for. . . Mr. Kilcoyne," Kelsey said carefully.

"A fence is generally accepted as evidence of trespass."

She sighed inwardly. Maybe she should have guessed that Crazy Joe would be the one person in Whiskey River who would be adamant about trespassing. For anyone else in town, a quick "Oops, sorry," or "I was looking for. . ." would suffice.

"Look, I'm sorry, but—"

"Don't be sorry. Just leave."

Her anger sparked anew. She eyed him up and down, the unkempt look, the ragged clothes. "How do I know *you're* not trespassing?"

"If I am, it's not your problem."

"Are you?"

He seemed vaguely amused at her perseverance, which added to her irritation. There was no need to be rude, after all. She was the aggrieved party here.

"I work here," he said after a moment.

"Oh."

Drat. Then he did have the right to order her off. But she wasn't going to go just yet.

"Is Mr. Kilcoyne here? I need to talk to him about. . . some property he recently acquired."

"He doesn't talk to people who are uninvited."

She sighed, audibly this time. "And how do I get invited?"

"You don't."

"Who does?" she asked, wondering just how much of a hermit Kilcoyne was.

She thought she saw a muscle in the man's jaw twitch. "No one. Now leave."

He didn't say "Or else," but she knew it was implicit. And wondered why she'd first thought this guy was kind of attractive; his attitude surely wasn't.

She gave it a final, urgent try. "Mr. Kilcoyne's men are tearing down my house. If anything, *they're* guilty of trespassing. Not to mention pawing through my property, without permission."

"Are you accusing them of stealing?"

"No," she had to admit. "But that's not the point."

"What is, if the property has been sold?"

"Common decency," she snapped. "He could have at least given me time to find someplace for the horses."

One brow lifted. Only one, in that way she'd annoyingly never been able to do herself. "I thought it was your house you came about."

She waved a hand. "I'll find a place. But it's not so easy to relocate six horses, especially when a couple of them need special care."

"So you're not worried about yourself, just the horses." He said it flatly, not even in a questioning tone.

"Of course I'm worried about myself. I'm apparently being evicted with no notice. Which I'm sure isn't exactly legal either, for that matter," she added. "But the horses come first."

"Do they."

His inflectionless tone was starting to wear on her. Still, she tried for a politer tone; after all, he couldn't help his boss's orders. "I wouldn't be in horse rescue if I didn't feel that way."

It also suddenly occurred to her that she was standing here arguing with a man who was, for all she knew, the gardener, janitor, or who knew what other position far removed from his boss. But if Kilcoyne wouldn't see her, she didn't know what to do. Maybe she should just park her truck under the window where she'd seen someone earlier, and crank up the radio. Something very loud and very obnoxious maybe.

"Is he sick?"

The man blinked. "What?"

She'd startled him out of the inflectionless tone, anyway. "Just wondering if he's ill or something. I wouldn't want to feel bad if I blast my radio under his window until he comes out and talks to me like a normal human being."

His expression shifted then. It became something she could only describe as bitter, and his eyes went even icier.

"There is nothing at all normal about him. Now get out."

She suddenly didn't want to take this any further, not with this man. The way he was looking at her was more than intimidating, it was a bit scary. Yes, he was nice enough looking—okay, better than nice—but she didn't like his demeanor at all. And he did have those garden clippers in his pocket.

"I'll go. But you tell your boss if one of my horses picks up even a scratch because of this, I'll be holding him responsible."

The man opened his mouth as if to speak, then stopped. He just stood there, glaring at her, until she turned and walked as fast as she could back the way she had come. Only once did she glance back over her shoulder, to see the man had done the same.

Well, that certainly accomplished nothing. She got back in her truck.

By the time she got back to the gate she'd used, her anger had faded completely. She was unable to even hang onto irritation at the rude handyman or whoever he was. Although, if he was the gardener, as the clippers hinted, she had to give him credit for keeping that beautiful setting in shape;

it looked incredibly labor-intensive.

She felt a sudden wave of weariness as she got back in her truck after securing the gate. She sat with her forehead resting on the steering wheel for a long time, trying to fight off the emotion threatening to swamp her. She hated feeling helpless. It was something she had tried to ban from her life since childhood. But it seemed overwhelming in this moment, and she couldn't even think of where to start.

Only one thing made sense to her at this moment. She needed to talk to the person who had taught her the most about not giving in to helplessness and hopelessness. Who had shown her how to rise above even the harshest tide. Who had shown her by example what simple perseverance could accomplish.

So she would call her mom.

FROM UP HERE in the tower, Kilcoyne could see a great distance. Out over the hill country that surrounded him. From the east window, he could see the river. From the north, there was a wide swath of the hills. The south window looked out toward town. But more importantly, from this window he could almost see to his neighbor's place. The place where a crew no doubt already had that pitiful excuse for a cabin torn down.

His gaze snagged on something out of place. He walked

over to the east window where he kept a spotting scope on a tripod to watch the river—flash floods weren't unheard of—and picked it up. He went back, set it down at the south window and bent to the eyepiece, focusing the scope on what he'd seen.

It was the truck that had just left here. Stopped at the far fence line. So that was how she'd gotten in. He'd have to have that gate taken out altogether.

He straightened up. Watched as she got out of the truck. Some part of his brain, the primitive part he'd never managed to smother, registered the feminine curve of her in the snug jeans and t-shirt, even at this distance. The way she walked only emphasized it, yet she handled the heavy gate with an ease that spoke of fitness.

She unfastened it, drove through, then got out and secured it. At least she did that, he thought. But then, he'd expect that of someone who knew about livestock. He didn't doubt she did. What he doubted was that anybody could really care as much as she seemed to. More for the horses she took in than herself.

But then he'd never been much of a believer in human kindness.

He knew, for example, that he was called "Crazy Joe" by many in Whiskey River. Typical of people to call anyone who didn't quite fit their norms crazy. But he didn't mind. If it would get people to leave him alone, he'd take being called a lot worse. Gladly. He—

The truck wasn't moving.

She'd refastened the gate, gotten back in the driver's seat of the truck, but now it was just. . . sitting there.

He frowned. Moved to the left edge of the window and zoomed in on the scope. The angle still wasn't perfect, but from the slant of her head and the way her hair was falling forward, it appeared she was resting her head on the steering wheel of the truck.

He jerked away from the image. He recognized too well that slump of the shoulders, the posture in general. Helplessness was a feeling he was far too familiar with.

His stomach knotted at the idea he'd done that to someone. That, of all things.

He turned his back on the window. It wasn't his doing. If she'd stayed home a little longer, and not gone off half-cocked, she would have found out what was really happening.

You could have just told her.

No. He answered that voice in his head. *No, I couldn't. That would have turned into a long, involved conversation and I was in no mood.*

That he was never in the mood for extended human contact was something he acknowledged even as he shoved it back in the cage where it lived in his head.

Enough. He'd wasted enough time today. He needed to get busy. He had to figure out what to do next.

When in doubt, kill someone off.

His mouth twisted at the oft-quoted advice.

He knew how to kill someone. He just wasn't sure how to explain how you did that without losing your soul in the process.

Chapter Four

"DO YOU WANT me to come? I could fly out in the morning."

And she would, Kelsey knew. Lisa Blaine might be a star in the cutthroat world of California law firms, but she was a mother first and, if her only child needed her, she would drop everything in a heartbeat. This had been the core of Kelsey's life for as long as she could remember. And if she ever had children of her own, she vowed they would have that same certainty.

But they would have a father, too. For knowing your father had adored you from twelve years of precious memories, and knowing what kind of man he'd been by the simple fact that your smart, strong, generous mother loved him to this day, did not make up for his absence.

"No, Mom, you don't need to do that," Kelsey said as she leaned back in the diner booth she had to herself, stirring the coffee she had barely taken a sip of.

"I didn't ask if I needed to, just if you wanted me to."

"I love you for offering, but I'll handle it. I just needed

to. . . vent, I guess."

"I'd be happy to come out there and give that man what for," her mom said. "Messing with you and the good work you're doing like that."

And that would be a sight to see. Her mother coming up against Crazy Joe. Even if he was truly nuts, she'd put her money on her mother any time. And that grumpy gardener wouldn't stand a chance, either; when it came to standing up for her daughter, Lisa Blaine was a force of nature.

Even when Kelsey had decided to leave a promising advertising career to come back to her father's Texas and devote her life to the horses she loved, her mother had supported her. "If I hadn't followed my heart with your father, I wouldn't have you," she'd said. And no matter the pain that that had brought her, with him first missing in action and then coming home in a flag-draped coffin, Kelsey knew her mother meant the words completely.

"As much as I'd love to watch that encounter, no," she said.

"Well, if you won't let me come out and knock some sense into him, what are you going to do?"

"Given he won't even talk to me—or anyone, apparently—I'm not sure."

"He must talk to someone."

"Not that I can find," she said.

"You said a trust bought the property?"

"Yes, and Crazy Joe's behind the trust, if Mrs. Murray is

right."

"She talks too much," her mother said dryly. "And she'll end up in legal trouble if she's not careful."

"I wouldn't trust her with anything I wanted kept secret," Kelsey agreed with a laugh. She already felt better.

"Do you want me to see what I can find out about that trust? If they deal primarily in real estate, I might know someone—"

"Who knows someone who knows something." Kelsey finished for her, knowing her mother, as a specialist in estate planning, had an extensive and varied network. If Kelsey had learned anything from watching this dynamo who had birthed her, it was that paying it forward and backward worked.

"Exactly."

"Yes, please," Kelsey said, deciding it couldn't hurt to know the enemy, and it would give her mother something to do to help. She'd also learned that from watching her mother deal with the aftermath of her father's death.

Sometimes the only thing you can do for people who are hurting along with you is let them help. Let them feel they've done something.

This was hardly the catastrophic situation that had been, but the principle still held.

"I worry about you, honey. That you're not taking care of yourself. You spend everything on the horses."

"I'm okay. It's tight but I'm making it." *Or at least, I was.*

"I could loan you some money to tide you over until this is resolved," her mother began.

"Don't even start," Kelsey said quickly. Her mother could afford it, but that wasn't the point.

"All right." She heard the smile that came into her mother's voice as she added, "Although, I know you'll change your mind if it comes down to the horses needing food or care."

"You know me too well, mom."

"And love you better."

"I know. I love you, too."

She put down her phone and took a long drink of coffee. Between the hit of caffeine and talking to her mom, she was already feeling better. Maybe even good enough to tackle ol' Crazy Joe again. There had to be a way to get the man to at least talk to her. Maybe she'd stop by the real estate office and talk to Megan. Kelsey knew Megan would be bound by the terms of the deal—which seemed to be total secrecy—and was much less likely to let something slip like Mrs. Murray, but Kelsey might learn something that would at least give her a direction to go. And she would know the rental market, and if there was anything suitable available, although Kelsey doubted anything would be within her tiny budget. She might be able to find housing for her, or for the horses, but not both together. And the horses came first, it was that simple.

Wouldn't be the first time I've slept in a barn. She turned the idea over in her mind and decided it was workable, if it came to that.

Decided now, she finished her plain coffee—the luxury of the fancier drinks had long ago fallen off her budget—and headed off to see Megan Clark. The woman was plugged into every aspect of Whiskey River, and she'd not only know if any stable or corral space was available, she'd also likely know if there was anyone Kelsey might be able to persuade they had something available, even if they hadn't really been looking.

And, if she got really desperate, she'd go to Trey Kelly. The owner of Kelly's Champs, the impressive, prize winning quarter horse producer, was always willing to help when it came to horses, but he'd already done so much she really didn't want to press him for more. She suspected he was behind that anonymous donation that had kept her going the last few months, although he denied it.

And she smiled at the thought of him, and how he'd changed since Ariana Wright had come into his life. Smiled, because it gave her hope.

She walked out of the diner and down toward the town square. The statue of Ronan "Booze" Kelly, loomed over all and, for a moment, she paused, as much to enjoy the sound of the fountain at its base as to look up at the image of the founder—however inadvertently—of Whiskey River.

She made her way to the real estate office, hoping she would find the industrious Megan inside. She got lucky; the petite brunette was standing beside her desk, on the phone. She spotted Kelsey immediately, smiled, and held up one finger to indicate it would be just a minute. It was closer to two—Kelsey could hear her assuring a client all was proceeding normally and she would have an answer for them soon—but when she hung up she shook her head and gave a wry grin.

"You'd think moving to Texas was some people's last salvation," she said.

"For some people, I think it is," Kelsey said with a smile.

Megan laughed, then gestured at a chair in front of her desk. Then, instead of taking her seat behind the desk, she sat in the other chair on the same side.

"Jim called me. You've had a rough day," the woman said sympathetically.

"I've had better."

"I'm really sorry, Kelsey. If I'd realized Jim had been too ill to tell you what was going on, I would have. At least you wouldn't have been taken by surprise by all this."

"Not your fault. Or Jim's." She grimaced. "Crazy Joe, on the other hand. . ."

Megan sighed. "I swear, it's impossible to keep a secret in this town. Let me guess, Mrs. Murray?"

"Got it in one."

"That woman," Megan said with a frown. "If she wasn't married to that county exec, she'd have been fired long ago. She couldn't keep a secret if her life depended on it."

"Speaking of secrets, what is it with Joe Kilcoyne? Have you ever even met the man?"

Megan shook her head. "I've talked to the administrator of the trust, who relayed information back and forth, but the man himself? No. I've never seen or spoken to him."

"Did you ever do a search on him?" Kelsey had thought about that herself, but her six year old laptop had finally given up the ghost a few months ago and a new one wasn't in the budget. She had to borrow a computer to get her photo work done when she had it. Also not in the budget was the data she'd eat up if she did much on her phone, without internet at home—

She didn't even have a home anymore. She interrupted her own thoughts, reminding herself of why she was really here.

"I did," Megan answered. "And there are more Joseph Kilcoynes than you might think. I found everything from a small time musician to a disbarred lawyer to a runaway teenager to a guy running for office somewhere in Canada."

"No serial killers?" Kelsey asked, only half-kidding.

Megan laughed. "Not a one. I thought maybe the musician, they can be. . . different, but he's pretty openly living in Nashville."

"The disbarred lawyer, then."

"I wondered, but this was in Chicago and there was no mention of him having any connection to Texas."

"Maybe he didn't, maybe he's just hiding out here."

"Could be. I couldn't find any photos, but I didn't spend a lot of time on it, since I've never seen the guy anyway."

Kelsey shrugged. It didn't really matter, she supposed, if Megan hadn't found the real guy.

"Never mind," she said. "I really came to see you about something else. Well, connected but not directly. Know anyone who might have a barn or some land they either want to or would be willing to rent out? Cheap?"

Megan frowned. "I'm sure there's something somewhere, but why?"

Kelsey blinked. "Since I'm going to need somewhere for the horses? A barn would be nice, since I'm likely going to be sleeping there myself for a while."

Megan's frown deepened. "Why on earth would you do that?"

It wasn't like Megan to be dense. So even though she didn't like sharing her circumstances with the world, she said flatly, "Because I can't afford both a barn and a roof for me."

"Then why are you moving at all?"

Surely the Whiskey River grapevine hadn't missed Megan. It was too darned efficient. And she'd brokered the darn deal with Kilcoyne, after all. But maybe she didn't know what his plans had been. And if she'd been busy this morning. . .

"Megan, he's bulldozing my house."

The woman's brows rose now. "Already?"

Already? She'd known this was coming? Over and above

the sale? She stared at the woman she'd always thought of as a friend, if not a soul-baring buddy. "You knew? You knew he was going to do this?"

"Of course, it was part of the deal, but—"

"Why didn't you tell me?" All the frustration of the day bubbled up into her voice.

It wasn't quite a shout, but felt painfully close. She tried to rein it in; it wasn't Megan's fault, after all. But still. . .

"Jim didn't tell you that, either?"

"He told me he'd had to sell the land. He didn't tell me I was going to be homeless by this afternoon!"

"Hardly homeless, when—"

"What would you call it when I come home and the bulldozers are already there? They went inside and packed up my things!"

"Well, that was rude. They could have waited for you."

Rude? *Rude?* That was the best she could do? What was *wrong* with people today?

"I don't have much, but that doesn't mean I like total strangers pawing through it all." *Including my underwear.* "They—"

The opening of the outer door cut her off. Teri Crane, a shopping bag from Kelly's Boots over one arm, came in and shut the door behind her.

"I thought I saw you in here," she exclaimed to Kelsey. "You sly thing! Why didn't you tell me?"

Kelsey couldn't think of a single thing in her life that

deserved that much pleased excitement.

"Tell you what?"

Teri laughed delightedly. "Please, you didn't think people wouldn't notice? I mean, I almost drove off the road when I went by."

Kelsey was suddenly weary. Of everything. "Notice what, Teri?" she asked, not caring if her words were flat and her voice sounded on the edge of angry.

"That you're getting a brand new house, of course!"

Chapter Five

"IT'S COMING ALONG." Kilcoyne paced the tower room as he spoke into the phone.

He shouldn't have answered, should have kept right on going toward the door. But David had been good to him, been his go between for a long time now, put up with his oddities, and so he had answered the call.

"I trust you. It's just that we're getting close."

We? If it's "we", then maybe you have an idea of how to get my boy out of this mess?

He didn't voice the thought. Having David worrying on top of his own panic wouldn't help matters any. Kilcoyne gave him a couple of routine assurances his heart wasn't in, and hoped the man didn't hear the decided lack of certainty he was feeling. He ended the call, tossed the phone down on his desk.

For the first time in a very long time, he wasn't sure he could do this anymore. And if he couldn't do this, what was left for him?

Total insanity, he concluded. Being a recluse was all well

and good when you had a purpose. Without that, you too easily slipped over into just plain crazy.

Crazy Joe.

It was already too close to the truth for his comfort. When he'd built this life here, he'd vowed never to let the outside world interfere. And he'd assumed it would take the rest of whatever natural life he allowed himself to get through all the debris he drug around with him. He'd also assumed the past would fuel him until he was done, that the driving force that had brought him this far would never fail until he'd exorcised every bit of it.

He'd apparently assumed wrong.

Because right now he was stuck. In a very, very bad place. With no idea of how to get out of it.

It was starting to look hopeless. And he was starting to feel helpless to change that. And if there was anything he'd sworn on his own blood he would never stand for again, it was feeling helpless. He'd vowed he would die first.

"So, here you are, Kilcoyne," he muttered aloud, long past caring that he talked to himself.

A lot. And occasionally answered himself. He figured as long as he didn't start arguing with himself, he was merely eccentric, not nuts.

He spun on his heel and walked to the window. He stared out over the hills. Spotted the gate in the far fence. Remembered he wanted to have somebody take that out altogether.

That thought make him think of the woman. Again.

She'd rattled his cage in a big way, showing up like that. So fierce, angry, and ready for a fight, only to let down into the dispirited figure he'd seen slumped against the steering wheel of her truck. Hopeless. Helpless.

Helpless.

The need to move, to do something, anything, suddenly erupted inside him. He slammed out of the tower room and ran down the curved stairway. And then he was heading down the stairs three steps at a time. He hit the back door still at a run, bursting into the outdoors as if it could save him.

But he knew nothing could.

"THAT'S WHAT I was trying to tell you," Megan said patiently.

Kelsey stared through the windshield in disbelief. She had thought Teri had mistakenly assumed that the mowing down of her ramshackle little cabin was something else, but there was no denying what was going on now. Several trucks had arrived, and there were at least twenty men working in various places, most of them where her little cabin had once stood. A few feet away, near the corral, sat a trailer that looked brand new. It looked more like a fancy house trailer than a construction trailer, but then there were a lot of workers here.

And, as she got out of the car, she saw what seemed like at least half of the inhabitants of Whiskey River who had a free Monday afternoon, all looking on with interest. She saw Juliette and Ariana, probably on their way to their lavender farm, Ryder Ford, the Kelly family attorney, standing near the open door of his car, with Wyatt Kelly himself on the other side, looking on curiously.

As they got closer to all the activity, Kelsey turned to Megan, utterly bewildered now. "Obviously, I shouldn't have left Jim to talk to his fishing buddies."

"Wow," Megan said, "what you must have been thinking, to come home to this and not have a clue! If I'd realized, I would have called you right away."

Kelsey frowned. "I still don't have a clue."

"It was in the deal, hon. The rescue stays right here. But that old, falling down place of yours doesn't."

"The horses stay?" Kelsey took in a deep, free breath for the first time since Jim's news had knocked her sideways. As long as the horses had a home, she would deal.

Jim's words ran through her mind. *You'll be fine, it'll end up being better. . .*

"Bless Jim," she whispered. "I should have known he wouldn't let them just turn the horses out."

"Actually," Megan said, "he didn't even have to ask. The trust's lawyer made it quite clear from the get they didn't want the rescue to be moved."

That surprised her. "Really? Some kind of tax write-off?"

"Such a cynic you are," Megan laughed. "The lawyer said the principal of the trust is a horse lover."

Kelsey blinked. "But. . . isn't the principal Crazy Joe?"

"I can neither confirm nor deny that allegation," Megan said in a very pompous voice, reminding Kelsey of the buyer's demand for secrecy. But then Megan grinned. "So, are you saying a crazy hermit can't be a horse lover?"

"Right now, I'm not saying anything. If I'd talked less and listened more I'd have saved myself a lot of panic."

"You did kind of go off half-cocked."

Kelsey whirled at the male voice behind them. She was embarrassed to see the man in the blue shirt she'd screeched at this morning.

"I was angry, because I didn't know—" She stopped herself. *Talk less, listen more.* "I'm sorry," she said instead, meaning it. "I did go off half-cocked. I don't, usually. And because I didn't know what was happening is no excuse."

"Didn't know?" the man asked.

"The seller became ill and was hospitalized," Megan explained, "and the details got lost in the confusion."

The man smiled at them then, and Kelsey thought he gave the petite Megan an appreciative once-over. And she realized he was really a nice looking man, tall, broad shouldered, with just a touch of gray at his temples, at odds with his younger appearing face.

He looked back at Kelsey and said, "Well, that explains

it. What I'd heard of you didn't fit with how you reacted."

Kelsey wasn't sure which part of that she should respond to, since it was both compliment and censure in one. And she was used to everyone knowing about everyone in Whiskey River. So she went with the one answer that would reinforce the former and hopefully make the latter.

"I truly apologize, Mister. . .?"

"Mahan. Truett Mahan. I'm the project manager on this." He held out a hand to her.

She took it. Strong, calloused, working hands. He hadn't always been a clipboard guy. She liked that.

"And nice to meet you in person, Ms. Crane," he added, with another look at Megan.

"I really am sorry, Mr. Mahan," Kelsey said.

"True, please. And apology accepted," he said. And then, unexpectedly, a grin creased his tanned face. "Although I would have liked to have seen you roaring up to the boss's house and chewing him out."

"He was safe enough, since he wouldn't even come out and talk to me."

True's brow furrowed. "But he—"

"Had every right, obviously." She hastened to assure him, given she was speaking of the man he apparently worked for. "I guess I owe him an apology too. Or at the least his gardener."

True's expression cleared. And he gave her an odd smile as he said, "Oh, met him did you?"

"If you want to call it that. I mean, I was upset, but he was downright rude."

"He has a way."

"I'll say." Her mouth quirked. "That apology's going to sting."

He studied her for a moment. "But you'll do it anyway?"

"I owe it," she said simply.

Truett Mahan's smile of approval warmed her, and she wasn't quite sure why, since they'd only just met. And not under ideal circumstances. Reminded now, she glanced around.

"Where did my stuff end up?"

"We put it inside," he said, gesturing at the trailer.

"Thank you. I'll move it. It must be in your way."

He looked puzzled. "That's why we put it inside. Didn't want anything to get damaged. You were already mad enough."

Her mouth twisted ruefully. She had been mad, madder than she could remember being since she'd seen poor Granite hobbling around on hooves that hadn't been trimmed in nearly a year.

"Anyway," he went on, "we figured we'd leave putting it away to you. Don't get too settled, though. House should be done in about eight to twelve weeks."

Kelsey blinked. "House?"

Megan laughed out loud. "For a very smart person, you're definitely lagging behind here, girlfriend." She looked at the man. Kelsey thought she saw. . . something in her friend's eyes, but she wasn't sure what. And Megan kept smiling. "You want to walk her through what's happening?"

"Sure." He held up a hand and started ticking off on his fingers. "Step one is done, obviously, remove that eyesore."

"I liked that eyesore," Kelsey protested.

It was true; it hadn't been much, but it had felt like hers and she knew all its quirks and idiosyncrasies.

"The trailer will be much better." He grinned. "It won't leak, anyway. Step two and three are done, too, we've hooked it up to power and the septic already, and they're doing the water now, so you should be good to go."

Kelsey blinked. "Wait, what?"

"Don't worry, it's only temporary," True assured her. "The construction noise will probably be a pain, especially with double shifts, but not much we can do about that. So then water is four, five we put in the foundation for the new place, six plumbing, seven electric, eight get the inspections. The modular house should arrive about then."

"House?" Kelsey asked faintly.

"Once it's here, it'll go fast. Couple-three weeks, with the extra manpower we put on. Get it set, hookups and finish work done, paint, and she'll be all yours. So you'll only be in the trailer a couple, maybe three months at the most, barring any major problems."

Kelsey felt like she'd walked in at the end of a meeting where everyone else was up to speed and she hadn't even found her seat yet. She wasn't used to feeling like this, so she wasn't sure how to act.

"When in doubt, verify your data," her mother always said.

"Let me get this right," she said slowly. "The plan is I live in that trailer while you all put up a new, modular house where my cabin was, and then I move into that?"

True smiled. "That's it. It's a nice model, too. I've seen it. Lots bigger than the old cabin, but not huge. And all your fixtures will be new, and you'll have an actual bathtub." He was grinning by now.

"I can't afford any of this," Kelsey pointed out bluntly.

True frowned. Looked at Megan questioningly.

"Kelsey, honey," she said in the tone one used to a child who hadn't quite caught on to the obvious yet, "you don't have to. This was all part of the deal. As long as you're running Whiskey River Rescue, and keep the horses here, it's yours. And it'll be a much better place to live in."

Kelsey knew she was gaping, but she was having trouble keeping up with the quick turn from seeming disaster to. . . whatever this was.

"But Jim was letting me stay here for next to nothing, I can't afford the rent on a brand new house. I couldn't afford the rent on that trailer, not and keep the horses fed."

"Well, the rent is going to change," True said, smiling as if he understood now.

"See?" Kelsey said to Megan. "I'd better get my stuff now and get out of here. I'll find someplace to crash and—"

Megan put a hand on her arm. "It's going down, Kelsey."

"Not next to nothing," True put in cheerfully. "Nothing. Now if you'll excuse me, I've got a couple things I need to check on."

Kelsey watched the man walk away, heard him whistling an intricate melody as he went. She turned to Megan.

"Nothing?"

"As long as you're running the rescue. Part of the deal," Megan repeated.

She stared at the woman. Remembered what she'd said in the office. "Crazy Joe?" she asked, incredulous.

"Maybe not so crazy," Megan said.

Kelsey looked back at the bare spot where the cabin had stood, and where the crew was already prepping the site. It all seemed so impossible. She still didn't quite believe it. But if it was true. . .

If it was true, she didn't have to just apologize to Crazy Joe, now she had to say thank you.

Chapter Six

H E MIGHT, THE gardener-pool boy-handyman thought, have pushed just a little too far today.

He slowed to a jog, finally having to admit that extra mile was going to take a toll. One part of him wanted to push through it, to ignore the twinge in his left ankle, the ache in his side. The saner part told him if he did, he'd end up flat on his back. Not that that didn't have a certain attraction right now. At least he'd have an excuse for not working. He needed a way out, and he wasn't even close to finding it.

As soon as the house was in sight he peeled off his shirt. And, in the habit he had never succeeded in breaking, he ran his fingers over the scars that wrapped around his rib cage.

Right. Think they're going to just disappear one day?

Angry at himself, he picked up the pace again right where he usually slowed to cool down a bit. His legs protested. He ignored it. He ran around the corner of the house. Hit the patio. Kept going. Paused only long enough to scrape off his shoes and socks. The clean, clear water of the pool beckoned. He hit it in a long, straight dive, nearly gasping at the chill of the water against his overheated skin. Later in the year, it would be like diving into a warm bathtub, but now it was still cool and the jolt he needed.

Perhaps not the healthiest thing, he thought as he swam down to the bottom. He'd read once about someone who'd died from the shock of jumping into icy water while overheated. Too bad this wasn't icy, that would solve his problem, wouldn't it? If they found him floating face down in this pool?

His thoughts hadn't veered in that direction in a very long time, and the warning bells went off in his head. He'd thought that beast fully vanquished, and that it reared its ugly face now told him he had to find a way out of this, and fast. Too bad the part of his brain that usually handled such things seemed to be on a permanent sabbatical.

He touched bottom, turned, and pushed off hard. He broke the surface and the momentum kept him going up out of the water past his shoulders. In the same movement he changed his trajectory and was ready to start into a steady stroke even as he came back down into the water.

He froze. Started to sink. Went under. Played back the surfacing in his head.

He resurfaced, thinking he had to have imagined it.

He hadn't.

The damned woman was there.

Treading water, he wiped at the excess dripping into his

eyes. Looked again. Still there.

"What the hell are you doing here?" he snapped.

"Trespassing again?" she suggested.

"That's obvious."

He stayed in the middle of the pool. He wasn't about to get out and put himself on display in front of her. But he automatically, as a longtime observer of life and people, noted her faded jeans, cowboy boots that were worn in a way that showed they were used as originally intended, and a t-shirt with a logo he couldn't read from here just above her left breast.

A nicely curved left breast. Matched by the right one. And a slim waist. Nice hips. And legs. Long, long legs.

End of cataloguing, idiot.

"I come in peace," she said.

He didn't smile. Just glared at her. He hadn't quite gotten his brain off that inventory yet. And that was a battle he wasn't used to fighting. He'd sworn off that aspect of life long ago.

"Really," she said. "I want to apologize."

Well, he hadn't expected that. "By trespassing again?"

"Whatever it takes. Because I am sorry."

"Fine. You apologized. Now get out."

She drew back slightly, but didn't retreat. His legs were letting him know they didn't appreciate all this treading water, after that extra mile.

"Apologies are pointless if they're not accepted."

He kept treading water. "It's accepted. Go."

"But I need to apologize to your boss, too. I made quite a noisy fuss."

"I noticed. I'll pass it on."

Would the woman never leave? That drowning possibility was starting to feel a bit real. On some level, he noted he didn't like the idea, so he supposed it was good to be past the momentary bit of grimness, but that didn't help his legs just now.

"I'd like to thank him, too."

He wanted to yell at her to get the hell out, but he wasn't sure he could spare the breath. Then what she'd said registered.

"Thank him?"

"Yes. For several things."

He gave in and swam to the side of the pool, lifting an arm up onto the decking and finally giving his legs the rest they were demanding. But he stayed in the water, half-afraid that if he tried to get out and stand up they'd go to jelly on him. He really should have re-thought that last mile. Five was enough.

"Is he here? He's not answering the door."

"There's a clue there," he muttered, slicking his hair back out of his eyes as he looked up at her.

"I'd like to thank him in person. I thought he might talk to me this time. Because I'm not. . ."

"Screaming like a banshee?" he suggested.

"I didn't scream. But I was angry. Because I didn't know—"

She cut herself off as wariness uncoiled in his gut. What exactly did she know now that she didn't know then? Possibilities raced through his mind, and he didn't like any of them.

"Didn't know what?" he finally asked.

She sighed. "My mother always taught me never to ruin a sincere apology with an excuse."

"My mother taught me apologies were for weaklings."

Now why the hell had he said that? He never, ever talked about his mother, and certainly not to complete strangers. And that this woman had been here once before—although maybe she hadn't truly reached banshee category—did not take her out of that category.

Then again, he had very few non-complete strangers in his life.

"Then I wouldn't trade you mothers," the woman said, and for a moment he thought he heard genuine sympathy in her voice. "Now, is he here, or not? I'm not leaving until I thank him."

He believed her. She wasn't going to give up. "Are you always so stubborn?"

"My mother also taught me that sometimes stubborn is the only thing that gets you through."

His jaw didn't actually drop, but it was a near thing as she spoke words he'd thought himself more times than he could count. It took him a moment to recover.

"Thank him for what?"

She sighed audibly, then seemed to give in. "For not evicting the rescue," she said. "For the house. And the trailer, for that matter. Not to mention the rent."

He'd started to frown at her first words, but understood by the last ones. "That's what you didn't know?"

"There was a. . . breakdown in communications that was nobody's fault. But no, I didn't know any of that until a little while ago."

"So you thought. . . what?"

"I thought the horses and I were evicted and my house was being bulldozed. Without notice."

Damn. No wonder she'd been in high dudgeon.

"So, you see why I want to both apologize and thank him."

"I'll tell him."

"Thanks but I'd rather tell him personally."

"He'd rather you didn't."

She blinked, and her brows lowered. "How can you be so sure? He did something incredibly generous. Surely, he wouldn't mind being thanked for it."

"He would."

"Why?"

"Because he doesn't talk to anyone."

"He obviously talks to you."

His mouth quirked before he could stop himself. *All the*

time.

"You don't really want to talk to him. Haven't you heard? He's crazy."

"Right. 'Crazy Joe.' I've heard. But if so, he's my kind of crazy. And even if he is, I still owe him thanks."

My kind of crazy.

In a twisted way, that was the nicest thing anyone had said about Kilcoyne in a long time.

And it was that that tipped him over the line he almost never crossed.

"Consider him thanked."

"But—"

"Personally."

He held her gaze. It was harder than he would have thought, and he realized it was more than just being out of practice. This woman unsettled him, and in a way he didn't like. He preferred to do his admiring of beautiful women from a safe distance.

He saw understanding dawn in her eyes. She'd gotten there more quickly than he'd expected.

"You," she said. "You're him."

"Just call me Crazy," he said, his tone wry.

Now he'd done it. And he still didn't quite understand why.

Chapter Seven

KELSEY SHOOK HER head in confusion. And a bit of embarrassment. She supposed he'd been amused at her before. Or maybe that explained his anger. "Why did you lie?"

"I didn't. I just let you think what you thought." He shrugged. "Besides, I am the gardener. Most of the time. And the pool boy. And the handyman."

Well, he had said he worked here, she thought before she said, "That's a lot of work."

"It keeps down the number of people I have to deal with."

She tried to imagine what it must be like to want to avoid people so much. She had reason, having seen what the more ignorant and blind of them could do to innocent animals, but she still believed most people, given the option, wanted to do the right thing.

Then again, she'd been accused of being naïve about that particular subject. And once it had led her down a romantic path that had ended in a very painful way.

When she realized she was thinking about Mason, she shook her head sharply; she hadn't gone there in a long time. Dwelling on her crash and burn was not something she allowed very often. And she had no idea why she was thinking about it now, when she should be thinking of how to extricate herself from this awkward situation. But if the man couldn't even be bothered to get out of the pool to talk to her—

Are you insane? The glimpse you got as he went into the pool wasn't enough?

She'd had barely enough time to register he had the lean, rangy runner's body she liked before he'd hit the water. And now she wondered why he bothered to run when he did all the physical labor the gardener here must do.

The gardener. And he'd let her go on thinking that. She tried to be mad about that, but considering how mad she'd been then, she supposed she couldn't blame him.

She realized abruptly she'd been standing silently—and staring—for too long a moment. It was hard to think when she was noticing how the pool water was beading up on his skin. And the way his left arm seemed to be at a slightly off-kilter angle that for some reason reminded her of Granite before the farrier had gone to work on him.

"Maybe you should just hire a person to deal with all the others," she said, as if she'd merely been thinking about an answer to his dealing with people remark. "Then you'd only have to deal with one."

"I don't trust anyone enough to have them around all the time."

He said it flatly, emotionlessly, as if he were stating a fact as obvious as the color of the sky. And then, for the second time, an expression flitted across his face that made her think he regretted saying it at all.

"I'm sorry," she said.

"You already apologized."

"I mean about whatever brought you to the point where you can't trust anyone."

"None of your business."

"True," she agreed, apparently surprising him. "I just hate to think of anyone living that way." He rolled his eyes, and she added dryly, "Even you."

"You don't know a damn thing about me, lady."

"I know that you have a temper, you garden, do repairs, and clean your own pool. Oh, and run. Lots of that, I'm guessing. In more ways than one."

She saw his jaw clench. Speculated a "Go to hell," was hovering behind those tightened lips. Wondered what it would be like to try and soften up that mouth.

Damn, girl, you'd better get out of here. You're skittering off into stupid land.

Making her tone as breezy as she could, she said, "My apologies again, my thanks again, and. . . you better get out of there before you shrivel up on the outside, too."

She turned her back on him and headed toward the corner of the house. She was three feet away before it hit her that last comment she'd thought so clever could be taken in quite another way. She heard the rush of water that told her he had done just that, gotten himself out of the pool.

Even as she told herself not to, she looked over her shoulder. Oh, yes, that body was just her type, rangy, leanly muscled but broad shouldered, and. . . marked. Scarred. What she saw jolted her. His back was to her as he walked toward the house. But she couldn't mistake the crisscross of marks on his back, even though they looked well-healed, even old. A couple of them wrapped around his side so far they almost reached the front. She knew her mouth was open in shock, but she couldn't help it.

And then he stopped in his tracks. Just froze, as if he somehow knew she was staring at him.

And then she realized he did know. Because he—and she—were fully reflected in the slightly mirrored coating of the tall windows of the house that looked out on the pool.

Beyond embarrassed, she turned away. And did her own running, back to her truck. And every step of the way her thoughts were warring, the unexpected and unwanted spark of interest, and the fact that he'd been utterly, totally right.

She didn't know a damn thing about him.

"YOU SOUND A little scattered, honey."

Kelsey had been walking aimlessly around the town square, past the drugstore, Riva's Java, past Megan's office again, and then the bookstore, when her cell had rung.

"Things are a little crazy, Mom."

"I can imagine. Have you found a place yet?"

"No. But now it seems I don't have to."

"What?"

She explained, ruefully admitting to, as True Mahan had said, going off half-cocked.

"Oh, boy," her mother said after expressing relief that she wasn't really going to be homeless. "Sounds like you have some fences to mend."

"Already tried. I apologized, and thanked him, but he wasn't overly receptive."

"Maybe he'll come around."

"I don't know. He's awfully. . . gruff."

"Maybe that's just a front," her mother said.

"Seemed pretty real when he was kicking me out."

She thought of telling her mother what she'd seen, but it seemed that would just be trespass piled upon trespass upon trespass, and she couldn't quite bring herself to do it. However the man had acquired those scars, it clearly wasn't something he wanted to talk about, or wanted talked about. Not given his purposeful isolation. And his demeanor, like that of a horse who'd been so mistreated he shied away from the gentlest hand.

Was that it? He was clearly wealthy enough to have

drawn attention from unsavory types, had it resulted in a kidnapping, complete with torture? Had he been held prisoner somewhere, and brutalized? She suppressed an inward shiver. She shouldn't even be pondering this. He'd gone to great lengths to set and keep himself apart, and it was only by chance that she'd seen as much as she had. He had a right to his privacy, and judging by those awful scars, good reason to want it. And she'd gone and trampled all over it, even if it was by accident.

It was in her nature to want to help any animal who had been abused, but she didn't have the know-how to help this one. Coaxing a frightened horse back to trust was one thing, trying to do the same to a clearly damaged and complex human being was something else altogether. She'd seen something she—or anyone—was never supposed to see, and she doubted he'd soon forgive her for that.

Even if she did think he was the sexiest thing she'd seen in a long time. She—

" . . . did learn something."

She snapped back to reality at her mother's words.

"What?"

"Nothing specific about him, I'm afraid. I can't tell you who he really is or anything."

"Of course not," Kelsey said with a rueful laugh. "That would be too easy. For all I know, he could be a criminal in hiding. Maybe he ran afoul of a rival drug lord or something." *Might explain the scars.*

Her mother let out a short chuckle. "Well, that would be a dramatic turn. I hope you didn't say that? Because I think you might have to apologize again if you did."

Kelsey laughed. "Of course not. And a good thing, since he barely accepted this one."

"Honey, you've done all you can do, at least for now. You've apologized, thanked him, now perhaps the best thing you can do for him is leave him in peace."

"I suppose. Although. . . I don't think he knows much about peace." Kelsey's mouth quirked. "Then again, as he bluntly told me, I don't know a damn thing about him."

"Sounds like an. . . interesting conversation. But back to what I learned, after looking into that trust that bought both the ranch and your property. He's hidden very deep, himself, so I can't even confirm it's really him. But the trust itself was set up three years ago, by a firm in New York City."

"He didn't strike me as a big city guy." Again his words echoed in her head, and she laughed at herself. "Boy, I make a lot of assumptions. Sorry, go ahead."

"Your instincts are generally good about people," her mother reassured her. "Anyway, that trust, besides buying those properties and some others, is also involved in supporting some charitable causes that make me think he's not really a bad guy. Unless, of course, he's not involved in any of the decision making."

"Interesting," Kelsey said.

"You'd like one of the other recipients, by the way. The

Mustang Fund."

Kelsey's eyes widened. She'd worked with the Mustang Fund, an organization dedicated to saving and preserving the dwindling numbers of wild horses across several states. In the last couple of years she'd taken in two that had been injured and unlikely to survive in the wild. The little buckskin mare, gentle by nature, had adapted quickly to her new life. She had ended up adopted by a family with a daughter who adored her at first sight and cared nothing about her slight lameness. Kelsey still saw them occasionally, and it always made her smile to think of how the sweet girl had landed safely in tall grass.

The big, roman-nosed bay had been another beast altogether, and she'd ended that one with some scars of her own before Trey Kelly had helped her find the perfect place for him through his half-brother Nick, the bull rider. Shouldering the big, sometimes testy bulls around suited the animal perfectly, and he took to the job quickly.

"Well, he gets definite points for that one, then, if he had anything to do with it," she told her mother.

"I thought you'd like that. My friend said there were several other horse related beneficiaries, some kids and youth organizations, and libraries, that kind of thing."

"Good stuff."

"Yes."

Kelsey sighed. "Now I feel even worse about jumping the gun."

"Well," Lisa Blaine said supportively, "they were tearing down your house without even giving you a chance to pack yourself."

"At least I don't have your wardrobe to worry about." Kelsey teased; her mother had exquisite taste and a great eye for style, and had always managed to look professional and elegant even when she was on a much smaller budget than anyone would ever guess.

"I could help you with that, you know."

Her mother was ever hopeful she could get her daughter out of jeans and boots. "Not my life, mom. You know that."

"I also know you could increase your funding with a little effort at courting donors. What's that thing they do, Boots & Buckles?"

"You mean the charity ball? Boots and Bangles."

"Whichever."

"That raises money for the Kelly Foundation, and they already give enough."

"So you focus on others, then. With your looks, charm, and the right little black dress at that or some cattle or oil man's gala, and you'd have them writing checks with lots of zeroes."

"You mean, since I learned from a master?" Kelsey asked, knowing her smile was echoing in her voice.

Her mother had turned her grief into dynamic action, and agencies that helped the widows and children of fallen warriors had all done better since she had found that channel for emotions that had threatened to swamp them both.

Her mother laughed. "I'm just glad you apparently found a generous donor without even having to look. And that you'll have a roof over your head."

"More," Kelsey said. "I'll apparently even have a bathtub, when the house is in place."

"Ah, my little girl. You've done without so much to do what your heart tells you to do. I am so proud of you."

"Back at you, mother-mine. I've had the best example a girl could have on how to live through hell with grace."

There was a pause before her mother said, in a voice Kelsey rarely heard from her. "I think he would be proud of us both, Kelsey."

"I know he would, Mom. I know he would."

Kelsey sat for a long, quiet moment after the call ended, full of tangled emotions and a determination to live up to the two examples she'd had in her life; a man who had given everything to the country and people he loved, and a woman who had fought her own way through debilitating grief and loss to come out stronger, and a fighter in her own right.

And she remembered something suddenly, something her father had told her as a child, before he had left for deployment that last time. She'd been tearfully whining about Breanna down the street being so mean when her father had crouched before her, and said in a voice that always made her listen carefully, "Be careful about judging others, Kels. Because you don't know what they're carrying."

She'd only found out later that Breanna's sister had been diagnosed with a terminal cancer, ripping her young world apart.

Kelsey had apparently needed a refresher on that life lesson. She slipped her phone back into her hip pocket. The next time she encountered the likes of Crazy Joe Kilcoyne, she would remember.

Chapter Eight

JUST KILL HIM off. That's the easiest way out. And what a lesson it would be. That you can fight your way out of hell a dozen times over and still end up dead.

He shoved his chair back from the desk, and slapped the cover of the laptop closed. Resisted the temptation to heave it through the window, wondering if he could sail it all the way into the river from up here.

He hadn't accomplished anything all week. Actually, all month, but this week stood out as particularly bad. Not only had he not found a way out of the current predicament, there had been that whole thing with the horse rescue woman. That seemed to have set the tone for his entire week. She had unsettled him, and he hadn't been able to resettle ever since.

As good an excuse as any, he thought as he once more laced on his shoes.

He supposed he had accomplished that. He'd put fifty miles on these shoes this week. That was something.

Of course, he'd put those miles on his already unhappy ankle, too, and he was paying a higher price for that every day. But until he simply couldn't stand on it, running was the only thing that gave him any sort of peace. Because the kind of peace he used to get after a good, long day's work was as elusive as the solution to his problem.

This time he was barely down to the river before his leg began the steady ache radiating up from that ankle. This was the fastest it had happened yet; he hadn't even worked up a sweat. He tried to push through it, hoping the protesting joint would loosen up and go back to its intended purpose.

It did not. And just past the bend where the river curved and headed toward town, it gave out completely with a sharp, fiery pain. And he went head over heels with his own momentum.

He managed at the last second to tuck up and roll, and came out relatively unscathed. Except for the leg, of course. He sat up, rubbed at it, contemplated what it was going to feel like if he tried to stand up.

He heard water splashing and looked up. A sturdy looking gray horse was headed toward him, making its way easily through the fetlock deep shallows. The animal was solidly muscled, quarter horse probably, with that set of britches on him. The clean, fine lines of his head spoke of some good breeding, and the alert yet calm set of his ears made Kilcoyne guess at a temperament to match. The bridle he wore was plain, and the bit nothing more than a snaffle, further evidence that this was an easygoing sort of horse.

"Are you all right?"

His gaze snapped upward. The horse's rider was sliding off the animal's sleek, bare back.

She landed practically in front of him, giving him an up close view of sleek, bare legs below a pair of cutoff jeans.

Curved. Sleek, bare, and deliciously curved legs.

Before she could catch him gaping, he dutifully shifted his gaze to her face. Or tried; it seemed to snag a bit on very female hips, and again on the curves beneath the snug black t-shirt with short sleeves that covered only the very top of her shoulders. A t-shirt that seemed anything but plain when it clung to her curves.

He finally made it to her face. Some part of him had already recognized her, but that didn't stop him from groaning inwardly.

"You again," he muttered.

"And you'll notice I was not trespassing this time," she said, crouching beside him. "I was on the other side of the river when I saw you go down."

"So you naturally came running?"

"Of course. I was afraid you might be really hurt." She leaned back slightly, still crouched there, close, too close. "That was quite a tumble. Should I call for paramedics?"

"God, no." But it did hurt. Really hurt. Not that he was about to tell her that. "I'm fine. Just an old ankle problem."

"Mmm," she said noncommittally. "No serious bleeding that I can see."

"I said I'm fine." Why wouldn't she just leave, so he

could try to stand up?

"You didn't hit your head, did you?"

"No," he snapped.

"Break anything?"

"No!"

Why wasn't she leaving? Why did she keep prodding? Hadn't he been nasty enough to drive any sane person away, sending them hightailing it back to Whiskey River with the news that not only was Crazy Joe crazy, he was a foul-tempered bastard to boot?

"Might as well try to stand up then, see how it goes."

It was so close to his earlier thoughts that his gaze narrowed as he looked at her. Her eyes really were that blue. He'd wondered before if she wore tinted contacts, for them to be that perfect shade of Texas bluebonnet blue. But she was close enough now that he could see, and there was no faint line around the vivid iris to indicate the presence of lenses. And he could see because her sunglasses were pushed back atop her head, holding back wispy strands of sandy blonde hair that had broken free from the thick braid down her back.

"Need some help getting started?" she asked.

"I need to be left alone." He grated out.

"Then I'd think you'd be a bit more careful, so you don't end up needing the help of paramedics, doctors, nurses, and a zillion other medical personnel," she said sweetly.

He almost preferred the angry woman he'd first met. At

least he'd been certain he could drive that one away. This patient, unruffled woman who seemed determined to play good Samaritan was something else again. How could he make her go away if he couldn't even make her mad?

She stood, and held out a hand to him. As if she would be strong enough to just pull him to his feet. He stared at that hand. It was tanned, with long fingers tipped with nails trimmed short and a couple of small scars here and there. No delicate, pale skin or long, interfering nails for this woman. This was the hand of a woman who worked, physically.

Maybe she could pull him up on her own.

He wasn't about to test that thought.

Instead he rolled to one side and got his good leg under him. This essentially turned his back on her. That should do it. The woman who'd chewed him out that day wouldn't put up with that rudeness.

But she was also the woman who'd come back to apologize.

And to thank him.

It hit him then, just as he was pushing himself upright.

She thought she owed him.

Her patience and kindness to him now made sense. She knew now he was, in essence, her landlord, so she was just acting like this because of that. Feeling almost relieved at the clearing of his confusion, he turned back to face her, glad he understood now.

Pain shot up from his ankle. His leg buckled. She

jumped forward. Grabbed him. Kept him from going down. And in the process he wound up in her arms, so close he could feel the heat of her, could smell the faint scent of lavender tinged with the indefinable and not unpleasant amalgamation of scents that to him said horse. It was an oddly intoxicating combination. That had to be the explanation for why his pulse picked up, his blood moving through him faster, as if to protect against another plunge into cool water.

Which was where he'd end up, if he didn't get himself on his own feet. Now.

But she was the only one around to grab until he got his balance back. And so he did, but he carefully grabbed her left shoulder to steady himself. It should not have amplified the effect. It was only a shoulder . . . it should not have kicked his heart into high gear, sending his blood racing now.

"Steady," she said.

And she was, he thought inanely. Solid, steady, fully capable of keeping him upright. Which had to be the craziest thought Crazy Joe had ever had.

And then he realized it had been advice to him, not a description of herself.

At least you didn't say it.

Sometimes the only things that saved you were the things you didn't do. Too bad he couldn't apply that to his boy. Him not doing anything would certainly be the easiest solution.

"Where did you go just now?"

His gaze snapped back to her face. She looked genuinely curious. "No place useful," he muttered.

She laughed. It was a wonderful, light hearted sound that seemed to wrap around him almost as her arms had. "Must it be useful?" she asked.

He didn't know what to say, so he said nothing. The sound of that laugh seemed to have stolen his voice anyway.

"You should probably get some ice on that ankle."

He stayed silent. Rubbed at the offending joint, only now realizing the pain had spread all the way up into his thigh now. He was in for a bad one this time. And he didn't want anyone witnessing it. Especially not her.

"I'd suggest just soaking it in the river, but it's really not cold enough this time of year."

"Speaking of rivers, shouldn't you be back on the other side of this one?"

"So, what, you're just going to walk back, on that leg?"

She had him there. He'd never make it.

"Is there anyone at your place that could come for you?"

"No."

He said it flatly, almost angrily, but she merely looked thoughtful. "I could go back to my place and get my truck and come back. Unless. . ." She looked at him speculatively. "Can you ride?"

His gaze flicked to the gray horse who stood peacefully, one hind leg propped on the point of his hoof as if he were dozing. Maybe he was, his eyes were half-closed. Calm wasn't the word for it.

"You mean now, or ever?" he muttered.

"At this point, I mean whichever you'll answer."

She didn't sound in the least bit perturbed, and for some reason that perturbed him.

"Look, you don't need to be nice to me now just because you found out I'm your landlord."

She looked startled, then thoughtful again. "I can see where you might think that, but it has nothing to do with it."

"Right."

"What it has to do with is something my father taught me a long time ago, about not judging strangers because you never know what burden they're carrying."

"What's your father, a preacher?"

"My father," she said quietly, "was a brave, decent man who loved my mother and me and the country he died for."

The simple words stabbed at him. There was such love in her voice, such sadness, that his own misery faded a little. How much worse than anything he'd been through would it be to have a parent you loved so much only to lose him?

That's why love is a fool's game. The price is too high.

But he still felt badly that he'd unintentionally caused her pain. He wanted her to leave, wanted her to stay away, but he hadn't wanted to hurt her. Which was odd in itself, because he usually didn't worry about what people thought or felt as long as they left him alone.

"Sorry," he muttered, not knowing what else to say. And since he wasn't sure himself, he left it to her to decide if he meant for her loss or for what he'd said. "I can ride. Not sure I could get on him, though."

"I'll give you a leg up." At his look she laughed again. "I can toss a hundred pound bale of hay, so I think I can give you a two-second lift. Think you can get the bad leg over his back?"

He tested it by trying to raise his leg now. It didn't seem too bad. It was putting weight on it that made it scream. He nodded.

"Good. Let's get you aboard, then you can give me a hand up, and we'll get you home."

Belatedly it hit him that he'd just agreed to riding double with this woman who had so unsettled him. And that he didn't see any other options only made it worse.

Because he'd sworn long ago that he would never again be in a position where he had no choice.

Chapter Nine

"GRANITE COULD EMPATHIZE with you," Kelsey said. Probably silly, but she felt the need to say something. Riding double bareback was a rather more intimate thing than in a saddle where you had a leather barrier between you, and if you were the back rider you were more concerned about sliding right off the horse's rump than anything else. But bareback, she ended up tight against him, her thighs open and his backside between them.

And he had, she admitted, a very nice backside.

She tried to divert her own unruly thoughts. He hadn't lied about being able to ride. He seemed perfectly at home, and when she'd told him Granite needed only a very delicate touch, he'd handled the reins just that way, although his left hand was at a rather odd angle. But it worked, and the horse settled easily into a collected walk.

"He belonged to some city couple who bought him because they thought they needed a horse to complete their décor. They never realized there was more to taking care of a horse than just parking him in a pasture."

He muttered something she thought sounded like "Idiots." She couldn't argue with that. And at least he was listening.

"He could barely walk when I found him. His hooves hadn't been trimmed since they'd had him. They had no idea hooves grew."

"Should have bought a plastic flamingo," he said.

She laughed, pleased. "I'm afraid I said exactly that to them."

"Good for you."

His voice was gruff, but it was the nicest thing he'd said to her yet, so she counted it as great progress.

"Thank you. Anyway, his tendons were all out of whack and inflamed, and it took a long time and a lot of work and care from a really great farrier to get him back to where he could walk normally. But he's in good shape now, as long as I don't work him too hard. Only the occasional flare up."

"I know the feeling."

"So I gather," she said.

He leaned forward then, and the flexing of muscle between her thighs brought back in a rush the intimacy of their position. She was glad she was behind him then, at least he couldn't see her face, which she was sure was a rosy red now. And then she realized he had moved to pat Granite's neck, and an entirely different sort of emotion filled her.

She spoke hurriedly, hoping her tangle of emotions didn't show in her voice. "I could put him up for adoption, he's well enough now, but he's just the sweetest horse, and I can't bring myself to do it."

"Why should you? He's alive and well because of you."

She knew what he meant, that many—too many in her view—would have had Granite put down rather than tackle the long, labor-intensive process of trying to save him. That such a wonderful, willing animal could have died because of the ignorance and indifference of people who shouldn't own a living creature did, as her Texas-born father used to say, chap her hide.

"Do you have horses?" she asked.

"No."

"But you have had?"

"Not since I was a kid."

"You should," she said. "Obviously you're good with them and you ride well."

"I'll never have another horse."

He said it flatly, and with a tone that made her wonder what was behind the finality of it. And made her curious; if he felt that way, then why the donations from his trust to various horse related charities? A possibility occurred to her, and while it was a bit personal to ask, he seemed to find it easier to talk when they weren't actually looking at each other.

"Did a horse hurt your leg? Is that why you won't have one?"

She felt him go tense. "Hardly. A human gets credit for

that."

She wondered who, and how, but sensed he was on the edge of shutting down all over again so didn't ask. Instead she changed the subject completely.

"I swear, sometimes I think I can smell the lavender farm out here, even though it's not very close."

He didn't respond.

"How far do you usually run?" she asked; she'd seen the faint trail running along the river, saw now that it appeared to continue along what she guessed was the property line. In fact, now that she thought about it, there was the same kind of faint foot trail just inside the fence at the gate she'd used to. . . trespass.

He didn't answer that, either, so she took the hint and occupied herself with wondering, if his running path ran around the entire perimeter of his property, how far that would be. And wishing Granite could move faster, but not even suggesting it because she didn't want to put the pressure of the extra weight on him at a gallop. Besides, Joe's leg might not be up to that.

And at a faster gait, they'd be rubbing together even more. This was bad enough, without adding that into the mix.

And what was "this"? What strange proclivity had she developed that she found the infamous "Crazy Joe" of Whiskey River crazily. . . appealing?

She didn't like even thinking the nickname the town had

given him. He wasn't crazy. Unconventional, maybe quirky, maybe even eccentric, but he wasn't crazy.

But he was still trouble. And her reaction to him was, simply, that she hadn't been on a date in eons. That had to explain it.

When they finally arrived at the big, sprawling house, he guided the horse to a door tucked into the stonework of the circular tower at the end of the house that overlooked the river. She'd not been around here before, but wasn't sure she'd have seen the door anyway, since it was half hidden by a large esperanza bush.

He pulled Granite to a halt at the stone walkway that curved around this side of the house. She slid off quickly to allow him room to maneuver his bad leg over the horse's back. She stayed close enough to help if he needed it, but he landed on his good leg and stayed balanced with a hand on Granite's withers.

"Good horse," he said when the gray stood quietly.

"He is."

"Worth it," he said, clearly referring to all the effort it had taken to bring the steady animal back to decent health.

"Yes."

She wondered why he had chosen this door, out of all of them on the house. Wondered what was inside this big, round, stone tower that looked like something out of not just a different era, but a different country. What sort of whimsy had made whoever it had been add this particular bit to the sprawling structure?

She glanced back, and realized she couldn't see anything of the rest of the house from where they stood.

"It really looks like a castle from here," she said.

"I prefer to think of it as a fortress."

For some reason, she thought about his comment on the sole blame for his leg. And she thought of all the people—herself included—who had so casually termed him Crazy Joe, and she wasn't very happy with any of them. Especially herself.

"Perhaps you should put in a moat," she suggested, making certain her tone made it impossible to sound like anything except a joke.

"Thought about it," he said. "But they told me the liability insurance for the alligators would cost millions."

She nearly gaped at him. Had he actually made a joke himself? Or was he serious? Either seemed possible. She caught the slightest of twitches at one corner of his mouth, and went with joke.

"Not to mention the upkeep," she said. "Have you seen the price of meat lately?"

Again the twitch of his mouth. "I could always feed them trespassers." He eyed her pointedly. "Not that you'd be much of a meal."

She wasn't sure how to take that one, either. Insult or compliment? But not for nothing had she been raised by a woman who could charm crusty four-star generals.

"But tasty," she said with an over-the-top batting of her eyelashes.

For an instant he just stared. Then he grimaced and turned his head away sharply. And that, she guessed, was the end of that. Oddly, she felt bad about that, he'd seemed almost normal for a moment, despite the tone of the teasing exchange.

Then again, maybe he'd been serious about the 'gators after all.

★

TASTY.

Oh, I'll just bet.

As he levered himself off the leather couch in his office, he shoved the image of her flashing that grin, fluttering her eyelashes at him in that obviously exaggerated way, out of his mind. But her words kept echoing in his head, and he wasn't having much luck shutting that up.

Tasty.

For the first time in a very long time, he thought about searching out someone to ease the need he usually kept buried deep. But he recoiled at the idea. He never wanted more than a casual hookup, never had, but right now even that was too much effort. Even that came with too many questions he didn't want to hear, let alone answer. And a pro was out of the question, as it always had been. While the impersonal nature of that kind of sexual contact appealed, the potential repercussions now did not.

His mouth tightened at the irony; when he would have done it, he couldn't afford it, now that he could he didn't dare.

He hobbled back to the small kitchenette in the far alcove, and opened the freezer for a fresh ice pack. He slipped it into the pocket of the wrap that went around his leg, wound it just above his ankle in the old, scarred spot, and secured the Velcro fastening. It was a familiar routine he didn't have to think much about. This was as bad as it had been in a long time, though. He tried to focus on that. If only to keep Kelsey Blaine out of his head.

And yet, when he was back at his desk, his aching ankle propped on top for elevation, instead of using some of his vaunted discipline and working, he found himself opening an old email. He told himself to stop, but the moment the window opened on his screen he knew he wouldn't. He scanned the report until his eye snagged on the name he was looking for.

Kelsey Erica Blaine.

As far as our inquiries went, Ms. Blaine appears to be exactly who she presents to be. We've confirmed her college credentials from UCSD, and her employment by San Diego Magazine. At this time, she assisted in the founding of a local horse rescue, and two years later came home to Texas and began the Whiskey River Rescue.

> *Father deceased (US Army, Captain, KIA in Iraq), mother lives in Redondo Beach, California. Mrs. Lisa Blaine, successful attorney, turned the income from Captain Eric Blaine's insurance and estate over to her daughter when she turned twenty-one.*
>
> *From our discreet inquiries, we believe that aside from very basic living expenses, that income goes entirely to run the rescue. Ms. Blaine takes nothing for herself, in fact appears to do without in order to provide for the animals in her care. There is no evidence of any mishandling or misuse of funds donated to the rescue. Her mother handles the accounting, and all documentation is in order. She applied last year for permits to open a riding camp for abused and neglected children, but that is currently on hold due to lack of funding.*
>
> *Ms. Blaine is well thought of, and appears dedicated to her cause.*

He leaned back in his chair, remembering the phone call that had followed that report.

"Would that everyone were as aboveboard as she is," Marcus Hanson, his long-time attorney and administrator of the trust had said. "In fact, I'm tempted to send in a donation myself. I'd like to see that camp happen. Using abused horses to get to abused kids is a great idea."

That, from Marcus, was the highest of praise. And so Whiskey River Rescue had been added to the list of organizations the Shipley Trust would donate to and support. And if

Marcus ever thought he went to extremes before adding anyone to that list, he never said so. The only thing he'd ever asked about the vetting process was, each time, "Same parameters?" So far, he'd never felt the need to change anything he'd set in place in the beginning.

And buying the land the Whiskey River Rescue sat on had from the beginning been part of the plan. But it seemed the lack of local secrecy was the weak link, as it had been when he'd bought this house. He'd thought buying this through the trust would solve that, but apparently not. Marcus had warned him about coming to a small town in the first place, but the smaller number of people to avoid had, to him, outweighed the potential for secrets coming out.

You misjudged that one.

He should have asked Ms. Kelsey Blaine how the hell she had found out he was her new landlord in the first place.

Chapter Ten

KELSEY LOOKED AROUND the sleek, modern interior of the trailer. It looked as new on the inside as it had on the outside. It was, by necessity, narrow, but it was cleverly arranged, with a living area in the front that had a big picture window bringing in bright light and making it seem larger. There was a small couch, two comfortable looking side chairs, and storage cabinets beneath the window. Beside the window, in the corner opposite the door, a flat screen television was mounted on the wall. Beneath it was a small desk and chair.

"Kitchen obviously is here," True Mahan said, gesturing to his right.

Kelsey wasn't much of a cook, but this compact, galley style room with shiny new appliances, including a surprisingly large refrigerator, might just have her doing it more often.

"Dishwasher's small, but efficient," True said.

To a woman who had hand washed the same plate, bowl, and mug every day since she'd moved into the cabin, this was a boon. Maybe she'd even get another set, and something more than a skillet and a saucepan to cook with.

"And on the other side, here," he said, taking a few steps to the left and pointing, "is the bathroom."

Kelsey stepped into the small but not cramped room. It was as sleekly fitted out as the kitchen.

"Hot water heater's right here," True said, "so you get it fast. It's big enough for probably a shower and a load of laundry at the same time, but I wouldn't push it beyond that. But it's a quick recovery unit, so you—" He stopped, looking at her no doubt stunned expression.

"Laundry?" she asked, rather faintly.

In answer he turned to a folding door opposite the bathroom and pulled it open. A small, stacked unit of washer and dryer gleamed inside. Kelsey gaped.

"Now you can change the doors here so the bathroom is accessible from either the living area or the bedroom," True explained.

Kelsey peeked into the room that took up the back of the trailer. It was another wonder of clever storage and arrangement, with drawers beneath the queen sized bed, and hanging closets on each side.

"It's small," True said, "but it has everything."

"Compared to the old cabin, it's a five star hotel," Kelsey said emphatically.

True smiled. "Boss said to go first class."

Back out in the living room, she looked around again. Some part of her brain, the logical, practical part trained up by her mother, was acknowledging that her power bill was going to soar.

"At least it's not winter," she muttered.

"It's better insulated than you might think. And it's got a good heating system," True said, startling her; she hadn't realized he was close enough to hear her. "And air conditioning, of course."

Kelsey blinked. "AC?"

"We tested it out." He assured her. "Got downright chilly in here."

Which sounded like heaven to someone who had sweltered through the past few Texas summers without.

"I'm sorry, I didn't mean to sound ungrateful, I was just. . .the cabin wasn't much, but neither were the utilities."

True laughed. "I'm not surprised. You had what, two outlets in the whole place? And that old hot plate probably drew twice as much as this whole range will. But in any case, not your problem. It's all covered by the trust."

She blinked again. "What?"

"The utility bills," True said patiently. "The cable's not hooked up yet, but you'll have internet and TV then. Should be next week."

She hadn't had internet at home since she'd been here. Or television. She had missed the former more, trying to run a rescue on her phone alone, with a minimal data allowance, had been beyond difficult. With a cable connection, she could do a better website, reach out further, maybe save more horses. And if she didn't have to pay the utilities, maybe she could get her old laptop fixed, or even get a newer one, so she could do all that, and work on her photos as well. Which in turn would bring in more cash.

She felt an odd weakness in her knees. She sank down on the couch, feeling strangely shivery.

"Ms. Blaine? Are you all right?"

"I. . . yes. This is just all a bit overwhelming. To go from thinking I was homeless to this in the space of a day. . ."

"You're shaking," he said, sitting down beside her.

She laughed, but even to her own ears it sounded weak. "Maybe I should have stopped for lunch."

"Speaking of food, we moved what you had in," True said.

"Not much," she said. "Cabin was a little short on storage space." *And I've been a little short on cash lately.*

"And we added a bit to it."

"You bought me food?"

"Boss did. He said to be sure you had everything you needed, since we were disrupting your life." He handed her a business card. "If you need anything, or have any questions about the trailer and how things work, call. My sister usually answers the landline, but if you get voice mail try my cell."

"That's surely above and beyond, for a project manager?"

He smiled at her. "I love horses, too. Oh, and in a couple of weeks we'll have the plans for the house for you to look at, so you can tell me if you want any changes. It's a stock manufactured, so we can't do a lot, but if you want a door or non-supporting wall moved, or added, that kind of thing we can do."

Kelsey was starting to feel a little numb. After he'd gone, she stood in the kitchen of her new home. After the old drabness of the cabin, she couldn't get over the sparkle. She thought about telling them to forget the new house, she could just live in this quite comfortably, although the old joke about them being tornado magnets did run through her head.

She heard a faint hum as the refrigerator came on. She walked over and pulled it open to marvel at the space after living out of a two cubic foot wonder that worked about half the time.

It was full.

Eggs, bacon, milk, lunch meats, a couple of steaks, ground beef, and several other things sat with her wrapped leftovers. Various condiments filled a door shelf. Bottled water gleamed on the shelf below that. It was more food than she'd had in her house at one time since. . . she couldn't remember when. This was a *bit* of food?

After that venture, she was almost afraid to look in the cupboards. But she did, and saw an assortment of staples and some packaged foods to be made on days that just ran too long. That made her go back to the fridge and look in the freezer. Sure enough, a stack of frozen dinners sat inside, neatly arranged so the labels could be read.

And a carton of ice cream. She nearly laughed aloud at that one. Someone had truly thought of everything. In fact, she was tempted to go for that first. She wondered where they'd put her meager collection of utensils, and started opening drawers. And found she had new flatware, cooking utensils, kitchen towels, a supply of storage bags, even trash bags.

She felt like crying again. And also uneasy. It was all just too much. Should she even accept all this?

The first bite of ice cream—she hadn't been able to resist rocky road, and if she felt too guilty she'd replace it—came straight out of the carton. As she savored it, she started looking for her bowl. And found an entire set of plain, white, but clearly new dishes.

Somehow that was the last straw. She sank down to sit on the shiny, spotless, cheerfully colored floor. This had been the second longest day of her life. Tears overflowed and ran down her cheeks. One hit the surface of the ice cream in the carton, and left a small circle.

She supposed it was better than crying in her beer, but she wasn't sure by how much.

Chapter Eleven

"I THINK SHE lives like a pauper so she can take better care of those horses," True said. "Her clothes fit in one box, she had no TV or internet, and there was barely any food in the place at all. And she got the shakes while I was showing her the trailer."

A sharp stab of painful memory shot through Kilcoyne. How often had he gone to bed hungry? That thought brought on another memory, of a burst of rage when, over one summer, he'd grown three inches and nothing fit him anymore. He knew she would have made him wear the jeans that would have flapped well above his ankles, if he'd been able to get into them.

And if she hadn't been afraid somebody would see the marks on his leg.

He yanked himself back to the present before the morass could suck him down into that pit.

"You handled the food?"

"Zee did," True said, referring to his sister, who ran his office. "And dishes and the like. She should be all set for a while."

"Good."

He didn't like to think of Kelsey—anybody, he corrected himself—going without food. That in her case it was for a cause might make it a choice, but it was one she shouldn't have to make.

And here he'd thought she was just stylishly slim, perhaps even dieted to stay that way. He'd certainly never thought that she was going hungry because she couldn't afford food. And from what True had said, he was willing to bet that those horses ate even if she didn't.

"I went back a few minutes later," True said, "because I'd forgotten to tell her about the hay delivery. She was sitting on the floor, with the ice cream, crying."

That image made him go all tight inside, in a way he couldn't quite put a name to.

"It's a good thing you're doing," True said quietly. "She's good people."

"It's the trust," he said dismissively. "Not me."

"Uh-huh."

Kilcoyne looked at the man who was one of the few he didn't mind horribly dealing with. But that was because he was generally a no-nonsense, all business kind of guy. Which he was not being now. What was it about Kelsey Blaine that had the man acting as if she were his sister too, or daughter or something?

The thought that the man might be thinking of her in

other ways sent a rush of feeling through Kilcoyne that he belatedly recognized as jealousy. True was a good-looking guy, if a bit older than Kelsey, but women sometimes went for that. And the guy had a fine eye. Although he was widowed and not inclined to partake, Kilcoyne reminded himself.

And what if he did? What if she was interested in turn? Why the hell should he care?

What was it about Kelsey Blaine that made it seemingly impossible for him to keep her out of his mind, keep her from intruding on his thoughts every time his mind strayed from his work, which lately had been all too often? It had to be more than simply that she was a smart, sunny, lovely woman with a great smile and obviously a generous heart. He'd run into those before.

Of course, their generosity didn't usually extend to dealing with him for long. He didn't blame them; why ruin your pleasant world with a cantankerous, disagreeable pain in the ass whose goal was to drive you away anyway?

"Keep me posted," he said to True. "Now excuse me, I've got work to do." *Don't I wish I could.*

But at least the man didn't quibble. He simply nodded and headed for the door. But before he stepped outside he spoke again. Kilcoyne stopped making his limping way toward the tower and turned back. Only then did he realize True hadn't been talking to him.

He was talking to Kelsey Blaine. She was standing on

Kilcoyne's doorstep, literally. And, damn True, he was just standing aside and letting her in. And smiling as he did it. And if he confronted the man, he'd probably laugh and say he couldn't imagine any man who wouldn't welcome a woman like her into his home.

He swore under his breath.

"How's the leg?" she asked.

"Fine," he snapped.

"Mmm."

He realized she'd seen him limping and knew it wasn't fine.

"Better," he amended. "It will be fine in another day or so."

"Good."

He should probably thank her for checking. That was what civilized people did, right? But then she might take it as encouragement to linger. "If that's all?" he suggested instead.

"Actually, it's not."

Damn. "What, then?"

She took a deep breath. It was the first sign he'd seen her give that she was at least wary of him. Maybe he needed to up the jerk amperage a bit.

"I wanted to thank you."

He scowled. "You already did that."

"I hadn't seen the inside of the trailer then."

"I didn't have anything to do with that."

"You told them to go first class."

Why did she make it sound like he'd done some amazing thing? "You're not going on vacation for a week in it; you're going to be living in it a couple of months."

"You had them buy food."

An image shot through his mind again, of her sitting on the floor crying into her ice cream. It tightened his throat so much he couldn't speak but only shrugged.

"A lot of food," she added. "Including a couple of beautiful steaks."

"Enjoy," he muttered, not sure what else to say.

She took another deep breath. "I'd enjoy it more with company. Let me fix dinner tomorrow night? I'm not a great cook, but with those steaks, you don't have to be."

It took him a moment to realize she meant him. As the company. He opened his mouth, and it was a toss-up as to whether a shouted *no* or a snort of laughter would come out. But somewhere deep down a tiny, dangerous kernel of warmth blossomed at the idea and that was warning enough to make him shut his mouth again without making a sound.

"Please," she said. "Then I'd feel I've really thanked you."

Did she have to sound so humble, so sincere? Nobody was that sincere.

Except, by all reports, this woman was.

He stared at her, wondering if he looked as stunned as he felt. "Hello? Crazy Joe, remember?"

"You're not crazy."

"Famous last words, volume one."

She laughed. "If you're trying to scare me, it's not working. Seven? Earlier if you want. You should see the trailer you bought."

"You would regret it."

"I'd regret more not at least doing something to thank you."

"I don't," he said carefully, "leave this place."

She drew back slightly. "Ever?"

"Never."

She stared at him in turn.

That had done it, he thought. "Rethinking Crazy Joe?"

Slowly, she shook her head. "I get the feeling you're many things, but I still don't believe you're crazy, Joe. Or Crazy Joe."

He nearly laughed, which stunned him all over again. Stunned him into stupidity, apparently, because that was the only thing that explained what came out of his mouth then.

"You're right. I'm not Joe at all. That was my father's name, and he may have hung it on me, but I don't—and won't—answer to it."

"I'm sorry." Her voice was soft with an understanding he thought impossible.

"For what?"

"For the way you feel about him."

My father was just a brave, decent man who loved my mother and me and the country he died for. . .

Her words rang in his head. He knew little of the kind of man she described, spoke of with such love and regret. He knew they existed, had even met one or two, but with one exception, he'd never had one in his life.

"My father was a shallow, self-centered man who couldn't have cared less about me or anything else except himself."

He saw something change in her expression, realized she'd noticed the echoing of her own words in the cadence and order of his.

"Is he dead?"

"Don't know. Don't care." *Don't know why I'm even still talking.*

"What about your mother?"

"My mother," he said, feeling the freeze start, "is none of your business."

"True," she said easily. "And I wasn't prying. Just hoping you had someone to balance out your father."

He would have laughed, but he was back in control now. The freeze that hit him any time he thought of the woman who had birthed him gave him that much, at least.

"Go."

"You truly won't come?"

Stubborn woman. "I do not leave." He repeated with emphasis.

She looked at him thoughtfully, then said, "You wouldn't really be leaving. You'd still be on your own property, after all. In fact, you could use the gate down by my place and never leave your own property even to get there. And I know you leave the house."

Well, that was an angle he hadn't thought of. He scrambled to think of an answer for a moment before he remembered he didn't have to. "No."

"Then I could bring it—"

"Just go."

Again that thoughtful look. "What are you afraid of?"

You.

The instant answer that snapped into his mind shocked him. And yet he knew it was true. She did scare him, he who had sworn he would never be scared again. That it was an entirely new and different kind of fear didn't ameliorate the fact. He fought it down by instinct, with a strength won only after a long and hard battle.

"It's a choice, not a response," he said flatly, hating the way her question had made him feel. Hating that she was right.

Finally, she gave it up. "Then just my thanks, again, will have to do I guess. So, thank you." She smiled, more nicely than he deserved. "The offer's open, if you change your mind."

He didn't answer. She headed for the door. He'd just started to risk breathing normally again when she looked back at him.

"If you're not Joe, what do you go by?"

"Declan," he said, the name slipping out unintentionally. He was still rattled, apparently. Or his control wasn't as complete as he'd hoped.

She smiled at him. The kernel of warmth he'd felt before burst into something a lot bigger, and warmer. Maybe even hot.

"I like it," was all she said, and then she was gone. Leaving him standing there, wondering what the hell had happened to twenty years of being able to control his slightest reaction to anyone and anything.

And how a single woman had managed to blast it to pieces.

Chapter Twelve

AFTER HER LONG but productive day, Kelsey stretched out comfortably on her new couch. She didn't quite understand why she was so. . . not tired, but relaxed. She couldn't be tired. Not after the way she'd slept last night.

She'd expected to be restless, first night in a new, strange place, but she'd slept for seven hours, straight through, for the first time in longer than she could remember.

Of course, she'd expected to be sleeping under just her old, worn blanket, too, since it hadn't even occurred to her that she needed sheets for the new, bigger bed. And then she'd found a brand new, still packaged set in one of the drawers under the bed, along with a blanket and a light-weight comforter, had made up the bed, taken a lovely, hot—not the almost warm she was used to—shower, and climbed in with a luxurious sigh. And, when she'd awakened, she'd felt energized, and had gotten more done today than she had in a single day in a long time. All the horses had had baths—and Cocoa needed it, with her tendency to splash water out of the trough just so she could roll around in the small patch of mud she created—which necessitated another quick shower for Kelsey herself. Then she'd done a photo shoot of three new cats and a litter of puppies at the county shelter and, although it was difficult, managed to escape without taking one home. After that she had spent a couple of hours on the free Wi-Fi at Riva's Java, working on those photos as best she could on the phone, sending them to the shelter, then checking email, paying bills, and answering what sounded like a genuine inquiry about adopting Cocoa, all while sipping a decadent latte she never would have dared spend the money on just days ago.

And all thanks to Crazy Joe.

Except Crazy Joe wasn't crazy, nor was he Joe.

Declan Kilcoyne.

She liked it. Wondered if it was part of his real name, or if he'd chosen it. Wondered why that name. Wondered what it was like to have a father who made him feel the way he did. Wondered about the mother who turned his eyes to ice.

Wondered why she was spending so much time thinking about it all. About him.

"How about because thanks to him you're in a cozy, comfortable, fully equipped place that's the Ritz compared to the cabin," she said aloud to the empty room.

She sat up, looked at the boxes still stacked inside the door. She hadn't unpacked anything but the necessities because she still wasn't sure about all this. She picked at a thread on her jeans, noticing that they were wearing so thin she was going to have to retire them soon, before they gave out on her in a very embarrassing way in public.

An image formed in her mind, of the first time she'd seen him, when she'd thought he was the unfriendly to the point of surly gardener, trying to eject her for trespassing. She remembered how his shirt had been faded, the cuffs of the long sleeves unraveling, the ripped and frayed jeans. She'd thought nothing of it then, when she'd assumed they were work clothes, but now that she knew he was the man behind the Shipley Trust, so obviously at least somewhat wealthy, she wasn't sure what to make of it.

She thought about finishing the book that was due back to the library this week, but didn't pick it up. She thought about opening the wine she'd bought, drinking a toast to the new abode. But drinking alone had never appealed, and she'd bought it mainly because she'd hoped he would say yes and come to dinner. And because she could only afford it because of him. Not that the bottle had been really expensive, but on her old budget it would have been out of reach.

Her old budget. Which now, apparently, didn't have to stretch to cover utilities or rent. And she still felt uneasy about that. Yes, she was running in essence a charity, but this place was benefiting her, not the horses.

She got up, began to walk around, still discovering the features of her new home. The part of her that was tired of living without was telling her loudly to just quit thinking and enjoy, but the bedrock core of her that had solid ideas of right and wrong wasn't convinced.

Maybe she'd call her mom. She always had good advice. And, after all, that solid core had come from her. Her mother would help her work out what to do, what was right. She walked to the end table and picked up her phone. The screen blinked the time at her, six forty. So not yet five in California. She'd still be at work, so Kelsey decided to text instead, knowing she'd get an auto response if her mother was in the midst of something that couldn't be disturbed.

"Hey, mom."

Less than a minute later, she heard the musical clip—a rising few notes of a Rachmaninoff piece that was her mother's favorite—announcing a return text.

"How are you? Sleep well in the new place?"

"Almost too well. 7 hours straight. Don't know why."

"Because it's been grinding on you, living like that, always worried about money. I'm so glad this has happened."

"I'm not even sure I should take it."

"Take what?"

"All of this."

"You absolutely should."

"It's too much."

"Obviously, the trust thinks it's a good investment. Maybe they'll use the trailer somewhere else when you're done with it."

She hadn't thought of that. Leave it to her mother to find a way to make this easier. Before she could respond another text came through.

"And anyone knows people are more productive when they're

not worried about their house falling in on them."

"But it's not just that. He stocked the whole thing, from eggs to bed sheets."

"He?"

Oops. She hadn't talked to her mom about that part. Nor had she told her about her futile venture back into Craz—Declan's domain yesterday. And she didn't want to go into it in texts. Wasn't sure she wanted to at all. Not while her thoughts were so chaotic.

"The trust," she sent quickly. She was standing there, phone in hand, hoping her mother would let it slide. For now, at least. It would only be a delay, but that was all she needed. Time to get her head straight. And get her mind to stop wandering to Declan Kilcoyne.

The image shot through her mind again, of him telling her his mother was none of her business. It wasn't what he'd said, which was true, but the way he'd looked when he'd said it. Closed down, shut off, and iced over. If his father was as bad as he'd said, what must his mother have been to have earned that? She reminded herself to tell her mother just how much she treasured her. She would call more often, too, she resolved, and not just with problems or for advice, but to say just that, how lucky she felt to have her. She would—

A new sound cut through her thoughts. It took her a second to realize it was a knock on her new door.

Saved by the knock, she thought, and texted quickly to her mother that someone was here.

"I'll wait until you find out who."

Kelsey smiled, and resisted texting back. *"This is Texas, not L.A., mom."*

The handle was a levered affair with two locks that took her a moment to manipulate, so between that and the phone she was distracted when she pulled it open.

Joe. Declan.

Her heart took a leap all out of proportion to his presence. She told herself it was simply surprise; she hadn't expected him to change his mind. It had nothing to do with the fact that he had taken some care, put on neat, black jeans and a lightweight, long-sleeved gray pullover. He'd even combed or brushed his hair, although she rather liked it the way she'd seen it before, all tousled on top where it was longer.

His eyes even looked different, taking on more of the gray of his shirt. They looked the color of storm clouds clearing out. Was his storm over? Had that been what all that was, some storm that had been tossing him, and nothing to do with her at all? Would serve her right, for assuming his mood had anything at all to do with her. And when had she started thinking in metaphors anyway?

His thick eyelashes were unusual, dark like his hair at the base, lighter at the tips, as if sun-touched. And long. Why was it that so many men had lashes like those naturally?

She yanked herself out of her foolish reverie. "Decided you wanted to see it after all? Come on in."

She pulled the door wider and stepped back as, without

speaking, he came up the three wooden steps bolted to the outside of the trailer.

Still saying nothing, he looked around. She saw his eyes moving quickly, taking in everything. Then, more slowly, he looked again. As if he were scanning quickly for threats the first time, but taking notes now.

Girl, you are losing it.

She'd never been prone to such fanciful thinking, and had no idea why it seemed to be overtaking her now.

Her phone let out those classical notes again. He looked at it.

"My mom," she explained. "We were texting when you knocked, so she's waiting to make sure it wasn't a serial killer at my door."

His gaze shot to her face. Then, with a downward quirk of his mouth, he said, "Depends who you ask."

So, he knew about that, too. She wondered how. She quickly sent an okay and a promise to call later, and signed off.

"She lives in L. A.," she said as she slipped the phone in her hip pocket. "Different world."

"Indeed."

For a moment they just stood there, awkwardly. And then it occurred to her she hadn't heard a vehicle. "How did you get here?"

"I used the gate, like you said."

She glanced down at his feet, saw he was wearing a pair

of black, serious looking athletic shoes. They were slightly dusty.

"You walked?"

"Just from the gate."

That was still a good hundred yards. "On your ankle?"

"Hard to do any other way." His tone was beyond dry.

"Oh, hush, you know what I mean," she said, but with a smile. "Shouldn't you still be resting it?"

He seemed unsure how to take her first words. After a moment he answered the question. "It's fine. It only takes a day or two."

He said it in the way of long experience. "So it really is an old injury?"

"Very old."

And that was that, she thought, from his tone. So she briskly changed the subject. "Come on, I'll give you the tour."

He followed silently as she led him around, showing him everything she'd discovered so far. She tried to sound grateful but not gushing. Spared a second to be thankful she'd made the bed this morning. And tried not to wonder what was in his mind as his gazed snagged for a moment on that bed.

"Will it work for you?" was all he said when they were done.

"Work? It's pure luxury."

He grimaced, looking around again. "That cabin must have been worse than I thought."

"It wasn't really that bad," she said, feeling compelled to defend Jim's place. She hesitated, then added in an awkward rush, "It's just that this is really nice. And a new house isn't necessary, really. This is really perfect. And then some."

"Really?"

She started to assure him with an echoed "Really," but realized he was looking at her with one brow raised. She heard her own words echoing in her head. And grinned.

"No. Four's my limit."

For an instant, she thought he almost smiled. At least the corners of his mouth twitched.

So there's a genuine person in there, she thought. All she had to do was dig him out.

Chapter Thirteen

H E WAS GOING to regret this.

He watched her start bustling around the kitchen, listened to her explain that it would be a bit because she hadn't expected him to change his mind. When he didn't speak she glanced at him, and he had to remind himself that it was customary to have conversation at times like this.

"You don't have to fuss." The urge to tell her to forget it and just leave was strong. But he'd made up his mind to do this, and so do it he would.

"Not fussing. Just fixing. I was going to do baked potatoes but they'd take too long, so. . ."

She paused, peering into a cupboard. After a moment he risked it.

"Microwave?"

Her head popped out from behind the cupboard door. She stared at him. And then she laughed, and it was a wonderful sound.

"Of course! I'm so used to not having one. You don't mind?"

"Mind. . . what?"

"Microwaved potatoes."

"I don't mind anything that's not frozen or out of a box, which is what I usually eat." He was startled at himself; that was a lot of words.

"Not much of a cook either, huh?"

He wanted to just shrug, but made himself say, "Not any kind of a cook."

"Too bad my mom's not here," she said as she pulled two indeed lovely steaks from the fridge. "She'd have a five course meal on the table in an hour, just with what's already here."

He had no idea what to say to that. He didn't know the first thing about normal parents. He should have thought this out beforehand, but he hadn't made the decision until an hour ago. He'd wrestled with it since dawn this morning, when he'd awoken after a confused dream in which Kelsey fought off the specters that usually haunted him, but then had turned on him to say that now she'd saved him, he had to leave. He'd groaned aloud at the blatancy of that one.

But he hadn't been able to put it out of his mind. And it wasn't like he had to venture out into town or anything. As she'd said, he wouldn't even be leaving his own property. Not really.

He almost smiled again at that last word. She was so open and. . . refreshing. Able to laugh at herself so easily.

In the end, even though he already knew she wasn't, he

lamely asked, "Is your mother a chef?"

"Mom? No. She could be, she's that good, but no. She's an estate attorney in California. Darn successful, I might add. Works with some really famous sorts, because she can make a will or trust ironclad. My mother is a force of nature."

So was mine.

He shook his head sharply. Kept his mouth shut. That woman had no place here, no place in his life or his mind anymore. That didn't stop her from invading now and then, despite his vigilance.

"So moms in general aren't off limits, just yours?"

In another person, he would have thought the words a dig. But her tone was light, and the question was uttered like a simple request for information.

"I don't talk about her."

She studied him for a moment. "You don't like even thinking about her, do you?"

His jaw tightened. But since he'd just been fighting that battle in his head, he couldn't deny that she'd somehow guessed right.

"I'm sorry. I wish everyone could be as lucky as I've been with my parents."

He blinked at that. "Your father died," he pointed out, he thought unnecessarily.

"But he was the best, and I had him for twelve years. And my mom still is the best."

She might as well have been speaking in Latin. In fact, he could have related more to Latin than the meaning of her English words. Again, he searched for something to say, even if it was wrong. Which it was.

"If she's so successful, why isn't she helping you out?"

She set down the knife she'd been using to slice a tomato, and he had the sudden thought he should be glad she had, rather than come at him with it. She turned to face him, and he tried desperately to think of something to say to change what he'd already said.

"I didn't mean to insult her—"

"You're footing the bill here. You have a right." Kelsey said.

He found he didn't like that she felt obligated to answer because of the circumstances.

"She offers. Every day. And she'd be on the next flight if I really needed her. I won't let her."

She turned back to the tomato, slicing now with a bit more speed. Probably regretting this too, wishing she'd never invited him.

"Why?" he asked, and he wasn't sure exactly what the question was really—that word again—related to.

"Because she raised me, taught me to be self-sufficient. By example, she showed me how to live. And I'm not going to live off her work."

"An independent sort."

"Yes." She smiled crookedly. "Until it comes to the horses. I'll take anything anyone wants to give when it comes to them." She gave him a sideways look. "But you know that."

He grabbed at the chance to depersonalize this. It suddenly seemed a crucial thing to do.

"Now you can focus just on the horses."

"Instead of a leaky roof, no heat or air conditioning, and walls that moved in any wind over about ten miles per hour?"

"I thought you said it wasn't that bad."

"Better than no roof or walls," she said as she finished tossing the salad. "Wine?"

"I don't drink."

She didn't seem upset, or even curious, just accepted his words. She carried two plates and silverware to the table, something he probably should have offered to do. He was even worse at this than he thought. And he was way past regretting he'd come. Wasn't even sure anymore—if he ever had been—why he had. But it would be too rude even for him to turn and walk out now.

You got yourself into this, deal with it.

The meal itself was good, the steaks were as good as they looked, the potatoes were nearly perfect, and the salad was crisp and refreshing. She kept up her end of the conversation easily, and he managed to ask enough questions about the rescue to keep her talking. But after a while it wasn't a struggle anymore; it was impossible not to be impressed with her commitment, knowledge, and energy. And the way she knew each horse's personality and quirks, and remembered every animal that had come through her hands. Her eyes grew suspiciously shiny when she spoke of the ones she'd been too late for, that had died or had to be put down.

"You'd save every needy horse in Texas if you could, wouldn't you?" he finally said.

"Of course. But I don't have to, there are other people out there doing what I do."

"I doubt anybody else is doing it with the same dedication."

She shook her head. "They are. Which is a good thing, because if I didn't know that, I doubt I'd get out of bed most days."

He hastily switched his gaze from her face down to his nearly empty plate, afraid she would read in his eyes what had leapt into his mind with that phrase.

What the hell is wrong with you?

He nearly laughed aloud at his own question. He knew exactly what was wrong with him. There were some parts of being alive that simply wouldn't be bargained with, and some needs that could only be tamped down for so long. And nothing like a beautiful, literal and figurative, girl next door to send those needs into overdrive.

Especially when he was stupid enough to let himself in for this on purpose.

"So," she said after a couple of minutes of silence that he found strained but that didn't seem to bother her, "You don't leave, you don't cook, you don't drink. What do you do?"

His gaze shot back to her face. There was nothing there of sarcasm, only genuine curiosity. A curiosity he couldn't give in to.

"Sit at home, most of the time."

"That's it?"

"I'm. . . I work on my computer."

"Telecommute, do you?"

"In a manner of speaking."

"When you're not running on a gimpy leg?"

"It's fine. The ankle just locks up now and then."

"What happened to it?"

"I don't—" He caught himself before he added another to her list. "I'd rather not talk about it."

"Fair enough," she said equably. "I broke my arm once, and it was so stupid I don't like talking about that."

"How—" Again he stopped himself, realizing it was hardly fair to ask, under the circumstances.

She smiled as if she'd heard his thoughts. "And you garden."

"Yeah."

"That's a full time job in itself, if you do all the work around your house."

"Most of it. I have people in for some of the big stuff, but I do the maintenance."

"It's beautiful."

"It's alive."

"A testament to your efforts."

"It keeps me out of trouble." *Most of the time. Except when I do stupid things like this.*

"My dad used to say it was good to get in trouble now and then. It's how we learn to decide if it's worth it."

I'm sorry, kid. If I don't get out of here, I'll kill her.

His father's words, issued with a pat on the shoulder that was about as demonstrative as his childhood had ever gotten, rarely entered his mind anymore. There had been a time when they were all he'd thought about, as he huddled in a corner, shivering with fear, trying not to cry, and wondering why his father wouldn't take him away with him.

The answer had come the moment his mother had realized what he was thinking. *Because who would want a stupid, useless kid like you with them?*

"I'm sorry."

The quiet words yanked him out of the morass. "What?"

"I'm sorry that my talking about my dad sent you. . . wherever you just went." She studied him for a moment before adding, "And I'm sorry you even have that place in your head."

He recoiled from the empathy in her voice. It weakened him, made him want to give in, to accept. Weakness lured the predators.

Even though he knew he was no longer prey, his reaction made his voice sharp. "I don't need your pity."

She sighed. "Sorrow and pity are not the same thing."

He stood up. "I told you, you would regret this."

"I don't," she said, slowly rising herself. "I'm sad you didn't have great parents, I'm sad you don't. . . participate in life much, but I don't regret asking you here or that you came. I owe you at least this much."

"You don't owe me anything."

"You get to decide that," she said. "But that doesn't change the fact that I think I do."

"Fine. We're even now, then."

"It's a start."

Meaning there'd be more? No. No way. She was too nice, too sweet, too luscious for the likes of him.

"Shall I give you a lift to the gate?" He blinked. "Granite hasn't had much to do today, we could ride."

Snugged up against her on the back of a horse again? Feeling her softness, her heat? No. Absolutely no. And he was going to get rid of that gate. He should have already. Didn't know why he hadn't.

When he didn't speak—because he couldn't—she said quietly, "You're obviously on the verge of bolting. Now, that is a pity, because there's a Banner's pecan pie for dessert." She'd picked it up at Banner Bread this morning, unable to resist her favorite treat.

He stared at her then. "Bolting?" And then, his tone accusatory, "You know."

Her expression of puzzlement gave him pause. He would

swear it was genuine. She didn't know what he meant. He'd jumped to a conclusion over what was a common enough phrase.

"Know what?"

"Never mind." He felt so foolish he sat back down.

"Pecan pie wins the day again," she said lightly, and he wondered what it would take to really rattle this woman.

And vowed he wouldn't be around her enough to find out.

Chapter Fourteen

WHOEVER CAME UP with the description of a riddle, wrapped in a mystery, inside an enigma—Churchill, maybe?—could have meant Declan Kilcoyne, Kelsey thought. The man was a tangle of all three.

No surprise, really, if his family had been as bad as she guessed it must have been. She had friends who didn't get along with their parents, but none of them had ever come close to reacting the way he did. If his reaction was a measure of how bad they'd been, some pretty nasty possibilities were occurring to her.

And there was nothing she could do about it. He'd made it pretty clear he didn't want any more contact with her when he'd left after dinner. Only the fact that it obviously wasn't just her, but people in general he didn't want anything to do with, prevented her from taking it too personally.

She gave a luxurious stretch, her new bed having given her a solid night's sleep for the third night in a row. She hadn't realized how bad the old twin mattress in the cabin had been. Not that she hadn't lain awake pondering that triad of confusion that was her neighbor and landlord and . . . what? Guy she was curious about? Guy she needed to keep on the right side of? Guy she was oddly attracted to?

She had just heard the first sound of the day's work beginning on the home site when a ping from her phone indicated a new email. She'd grown used to the first, but the ping still startled her. She wasn't yet used to being connected at home; she usually had to turn off all but the phone function so that she wouldn't go over her data cap. But the internet had been hooked up yesterday, and she could connect to her heart's content, yet another luxury courtesy of. . . that guy she was trying not to think about.

She took a quick look, saw it was from the woman over in Kerrville, who had found a case for her. Just what she needed, another horse to take in. But the tale was too sad to ignore and, if it were true, there was no way she could leave the animal in its current conditions. The photos she'd asked for were attached, but she didn't open them yet. She didn't want to be faced with that before she was even fully awake. She'd take a shower and have some breakfast first, and hope she didn't lose it when she saw what humans had done to one of the planet's most noble creatures.

The bathroom, even more than the kitchen, was her favorite part of her new, temporary abode. To have water that was actually hot, a shower big enough to turn around in without bumping the sides, and an actual power outlet beside the sink was a revelation. She was actually able to dry her hair in the bathroom instead of crouched on the floor of the living area next to the only outlet with a clear plug that could handle the draw.

And it was again thanks to that guy she was trying not to think about.

She scrambled two eggs and reveled in two slices of actual, real bacon and orange juice. Again thanks to that guy.

He's doing it for the rescue, not for you personally.

She had been chanting that as if it was a mantra and, despite being completely true, it didn't change the fact that she was the beneficiary whatever the intent.

She washed her dishes, by hand this time. It would take her a week—or another dinner with that guy—to fill up even the small dishwasher.

And finally she sat down to look at the photos the woman in Kerrville had sent.

She didn't lose her breakfast, but it was a close thing. The skinny, forlorn animal, head so low his nose was practically on the ground, his coat so dirty it was clear he'd been down in mud more than once, wrenched at her heart. The decision was made without any further pondering.

She dialed the woman, and kept the conversation brief.

"You're sure they're willing to give him up?"

"Absolutely," came the answer, "he was their mother's and she's gone now, and they haven't got a clue. I think they completely forgot about him until last week."

Kelsey didn't understand that any more than she did

cruelty, she thought as she locked up the trailer. When her father had been killed, she and her mother had treasured his big dog Max more than ever, because Eric Blaine had loved him.

She had filled up with gas yesterday, so the thirty-five miles or so to Kerrville was no problem. She'd need to stop by Kelly's Champs and borrow a trailer, though. Thankfully Trey was ever-helpful with that, telling her she could borrow one any time she needed it.

She turned to head for her truck and saw someone walking toward her from the construction area. True Mahan, sans clipboard this time.

"Heading out?" he asked.

She nodded. "Picking up a horse over in Kerrville, in bad shape, pretty much abandoned."

The man frowned. "I don't get people."

"Me, either," she agreed.

"Do you need any help? And will the workers spook him once you get him here?"

Her opinion of the man went up another notch at the genuine concern. "I don't know yet. I would tend to think not, he's more dispirited than skittish, judging by the pics. And he's pretty skinny, so he may not have the energy to fight."

"People," he said again, with a shake of his head. His frown deepened as he glanced at her truck. "How will you get him here?"

"I'm on my way to borrow a trailer."

"Borrow?"

"Trey Kelly. Kelly's Champs?"

He smiled. "Even I, the non-horse guy, have heard of them."

"Hard not to, in Whiskey River," she said with a grin, knowing it was true for not just Kelley's Champs but anybody named Kelly. "But he's great about loaning me a trailer whenever I need one. Keeps the overhead down if I don't have to rent one."

He nodded. "Listen, I forgot to tell you the other day, there'll be a load of hay coming in tomorrow."

She blinked. "What?"

"Hay," he repeated. "Looked like you were getting a little low, for six horses. And with another one coming in now, you'll need more."

She was always low, and it was always a close thing. "I. . . thank you."

"No problem. We should have the shelter for it done in time, I think. I put a couple more guys on it today."

She realized suddenly what that three-sided shed structure she'd noticed going up was for; she'd thought it was to shelter their equipment temporarily.

"Oh." She wondered how many thank-yous she'd have said by the time this was done. No matter, it wouldn't be enough. "Thank you again. And thanks for thinking of that."

"I didn't, the boss did."

That guy. Again.

"Then thank him for me," she said, since she doubted she'd be seeing him again to do so.

True looked at her thoughtfully. "Maybe you should do that yourself."

She laughed. "I think I'm persona non grata over there."

"I don't."

She blinked. "What?"

The man seemed to hesitate, then said, "Look, I've worked for him off and on for nearly five years now. I don't know why he is the way he is, why he chooses to live the way he does. Why he's cut himself off from everyone and everything."

She'd wondered that often enough herself, but the bottom line was still the same. "But it is his choice."

"Yes." He gave her a considering look. "What I do know is he does a lot of good things you never hear about, and he takes no credit for any of it."

She waved a hand back toward the trailer. "I've got firsthand experience with that."

"I'm just saying that in all that time I've never seen him. . . unsettled by anyone. Except you."

She nearly gaped. "Angry, yes. Irked, certainly. But unsettled?"

"Maybe he's angry and irked because you unsettle him." True grinned. "And that exhausts my supply of wisdom for the day. Good luck getting your new tenant here."

"Thanks," she said, yet again.

And chided herself as she drove that she should quit thinking about how many times she'd had to say that, and just appreciate that she had so much to be thankful for.

Mostly because of that guy.

Chapter Fifteen

*S*TALKER.

It wasn't the first time the word had popped into his head. It happened every time he could no longer resist the urge to leave his desk—where he wasn't getting anything done anyway—and go back to the south window and peer through the scope again.

The first time he'd had a legitimate concern, how she'd gotten onto his property. The second time, he'd been checking on the progress of the project, although he couldn't see many details from here even with the scope. But he could see the crew moving around, and the hay shed going up.

And the trailer.

Her trailer. With her inside it.

But he wasn't looking at it. Not really. He wasn't spying on her. Not that he could, anyway, it wasn't like he could see inside from here.

And now he was only checking to see if she was back yet. His conversation with True played back in his head.

"She's going to pick up a horse."

"How?" He hadn't admitted he'd watched her leave.

"She's borrowing a horse trailer."

That was something he hadn't thought of. He'd have to see about that. "She's going by herself?"

"She doesn't seem to think he'll be a problem."

She was, he thought now as he paced the office, taking a lot for granted. Any abused creature could be a problem, if it felt threatened enough. Frank Shipley could testify to that. The cop hadn't been seriously hurt, but only because he'd been so much bigger than he himself been at fourteen.

And he hadn't hurt the scared, cornered kid who came at him with a knife, either.

He shook off the memory that hadn't come at him for a long time. That just proved how rattled he was.

He just didn't want to see the horse, or her, end up hurt. Horses that hurt people ended up in worse places. Or dead. And while there would be guys from the work crew still around when she got back, most likely, he didn't know if any of them knew the first thing about horses.

But you do. . .

No. No way.

He went back to pacing, mentally listing all the reasons he wasn't going anywhere today. He had thinking to do. Never mind that he'd apparently run utterly dry. He couldn't even think of a decent way to kill someone who righteously deserved it. So what good was he anymore? Maybe the run of luck was over. Maybe he should just quit.

Maybe—

She was here.

For a moment he just stared out the window, watching as the truck with the two-horse trailer—the C and K of the Kelly's Champs logo emblazoned on the side—maneuvered up to the smaller corral closest to the trailer. She did a relatively proficient job of angling the trailer so that the ramp would come down directly into the corral once the gate was opened.

The guys on the crew paused in their work to watch. The thought occurred to him that this probably wasn't the first time; no breathing male could help at least glancing at a woman like Kelsey if she was around. When she got out of the truck a couple of them started walking toward her. She waved them off, appeared to call out something to them.

And he belatedly realized he'd ended up with his eye to the scope again, when he'd sworn not to. She hadn't made a move toward the trailer yet. She was leaving the animal there, perhaps to settle from the trip. She opened the corral gate, securing it so it wouldn't swing unexpectedly. He could see that she was talking, although the workers had retreated as she'd asked. And a darn good thing, too, or he'd have True on them.

It took him a moment to realize she was talking to the horse. Or for his benefit, anyway. Then she disappeared into the shed, which held a single horse stall and a tack and supply room, and which, True had told him, had been recently repaired and so was in better shape than the house had been, proving once more where her priorities were.

She came out with a bucket of. . . something, he couldn't tell from here. She was talking again as soon as she got close to the trailer. It was starting to get warm out, so she was going to have to get the horse out of there soon. This small trailer, unlike some of the big, multi-horse transports he'd seen, wasn't air conditioned.

She walked to the front of the trailer, where there was a small, narrow entry door. She set the bucket down, opened the access door, and sidled inside. Then she reached back for the bucket.

Nothing happened. He watched, glued to the eyepiece of the scope as if he were watching a moon landing or some once in a lifetime astronomical phenomenon.

Nothing.

Images piled up in his mind. Kelsey trapped, pinned, cornered. The fact that he couldn't hear from here only made it worse, made his imaginings fiercer.

He resisted. Clenched his jaw. Fought the urge.

And then he broke, heading for the tower elevator. He tried to talk himself out of it all the way down. When the door opened and he ran across the entryway floor to grab his keys, he was on some level hoping his ankle would act up again, giving him a reason not to do this.

It didn't.

It would be over by the time he got there, he told himself

as he drove the Jeep over the next rise, foregoing the dirt road. It would be over, she would be fine, and he could just turn around and come back before she ever even knew he'd been there. That was comforting.

He slowed as he neared the fence, the gate he kept meaning to take out. He could see the truck and trailer on the other side of the small corral. There was still no sign of her. The workmen weren't working. Tools had gone silent, no hammering, no sawing, nothing. But they weren't helping her. They were in fact gathered near the new hay shed, clearly taking a break, some drinking coffee, some sodas, some water.

He parked his Jeep, got out, worked the wire holding the gate closed loose and went through. He ran toward the trailer, vaguely aware his ankle was holding up to this, too.

He couldn't hear the sound of hooves from inside the trailer. Couldn't hear moaning. So she was either fine, or dead. Okay, maybe unconscious. He reached the back of the trailer. Only then did he hear it. A low, slow, loving sort of crooning.

"There you are, slowly now, my sweet boy. Oh, yes, your life has changed, even though you don't know it yet. But you will, and you'll learn to trust again, you'll have a herd, even though it's small, and you'll have someone to love you and take care of you, no more days alone, hungry, neglected, forgotten, yes, my boy, I promise you this."

Her voice fairly flowed over him, her words sent a shiver

through him, down deep in someplace long forgotten that had little to do with here and now.

He edged forward, not wanting to startle her or more importantly the horse, but not wanting to interrupt that sweet flow, either, for reasons he didn't want to analyze just now.

He could see her now, through the narrow door at the front curve of the trailer. She was sitting on the straw-covered floor, the bucket she'd brought at her side. Even as he looked she dipped into it and held out what looked like a handful of oats or some sort of mixed feed, all the while continuing that soft, gentle crooning.

An equine head came down. Muddy, scraped on one side, a filthy, tangled forelock masking one eye. A leather halter, trailing a lead rope, buckled beneath his jaw. Slowly the horse stretched toward the proffered food, hesitant, looking ready to shy at any moment. She held her hand steady, her voice coaxing, urging, so gently that Declan couldn't see how the horse resisted crawling into her lap.

And then he took it, lips brushing over her hand, taking up the handful of sweet feed as if it were manna from heaven. To the horse, perhaps it was. And she an angel, sent to save him.

The horse's head came up suddenly, and he whickered. In the instant he guessed the animal had scented him, Kelsey twisted to look over her shoulder. She was frowning slightly, and he suddenly realized she had probably told the workers to stay back, and stop working, so as not to spook the horse in his new surroundings.

She couldn't have looked more surprised when she recognized him. His mouth quirked.

No more surprised than I am.

"Want to let the ramp down for me?" she asked.

He moved closer, looked at the horse. He was a pitiful sight, skinny, dirty, woebegone. "You think he's ready?"

"He'd better be. It's getting too warm in here for him."

He moved back and unlatched the back of the trailer on both sides. He eased the heavy ramp down as quietly as he could. Then he stepped to one said, giving the horse a clear path.

At first the horse resisted, his nose reaching out toward the bucket.

"Oh, no, love, not too much sweet feed too fast, don't want you getting sick. But there's a nice flake of hay waiting for you, all yours, just back up for me, that's it, just a step at a time, easy now, that's my boy, a little more, that's it. . ."

As the horse backed out into the sunlight Declan felt his stomach knot. Skinny wasn't the word for it. Ribs, hipbones, withers, stood out like sharpened blades under a dull, red-roan coat. Another memory flashed through his mind, of himself looking into a mirror and seeing that same sort of bony, sunken image looking back at him with dull, dead eyes.

The horse barely glanced at him, listlessly. Every step he

took, as Kelsey led him a few more feet into the corral, was hesitant and looked almost painful. He glanced at the animal's feet, saw hooves overgrown and split.

"Blacksmith," he said.

"Yes. Tomorrow, after he's settled in a bit." She glanced at him. "I can afford it now. Thanks to you."

He brushed off the thanks with a shake of his head. "Vet?"

"This afternoon." She glanced at her watch, and he remembered noticing the utilitarian timepiece before. No flashy bangle for this woman. "In about a half-hour."

"You can afford him, too, right?"

He asked it before he even thought.

"Don't have to. Dr. Barrett is great about donating his time to us."

"Us?" Wasn't she the only one running this operation?

"Us," she repeated, gesturing toward the larger corral next to this one, where several horses stood, watching with interest. He recognized the big gray they'd ridden up from the river. A little, dark palomino that was the color of chocolate milk stood next to the gray. Beyond that were two bays, and then an elderly paint with a patch of brown over one eye. Finally a sorrel with a large chunk missing out of one ear.

Her herd.

So, of course to her, us meant them.

"Would you grab a handful of that hay for him? I want

him to go slow at first, handful at a time, but I don't want to let go of him just yet."

He had the hay in his hand before it hit him that he'd never even thought of refusing. Never thought of not helping with this poor, neglected creature.

He held it out. The horse tested it tentatively, as if still unsure what was happening, and if this was really food being offered, freely.

And then he grabbed at it, chomping with obvious eagerness. And then more, until the handful was gone. The horse nudged his hand, looking for more. He looked up at Kelsey.

"In a couple of minutes," she said. "I want to see how he does with this."

But she was smiling. Brilliantly. Happily. More like joyously.

And he realized what else he'd never thought of.

He'd never thought of running.

Chapter Sixteen

KELSEY WATCHED HIM feed the horse, one slow handful at a time. She wasn't sure which made her happier. She'd suspected from the time they'd ridden Granite that horses might be the way in. It wasn't that she was trying to worm her way into his life, just trying to lure him out into a life of his own that went beyond the walls of his self-named fortress. And why she cared about that, she wasn't sure.

She wanted to ask why he'd come, what he was doing over here, but was afraid to interrupt what was happening, for both their sakes. The horse stopped on his own about two-thirds of the way through the flake of hay, his shrunken stomach apparently full. She was glad they'd gone slow, although she'd have Dr. Barrett check his teeth to make sure there wasn't an issue.

"Full already, huh?" she heard Declan murmur to the animal. "That'll change."

She saw him reach out and rub under the horse's jaw, in that spot every horse she'd ever had loved to be rubbed. The horse nickered and lifted his head as if to make it easier. So he hadn't always been neglected.

"When did she die?" Declan asked without looking at her.

"Six months ago."

She saw him glance down at the overgrown hooves. "Looks about right."

Not for the first time, she wondered where he'd grown up, if that was where he'd learned about horses. But she didn't want to derail this tentative communication, so she said only, "I think she took good care of him. That will make it easier."

"He's not shy. Not skittish, just cautious."

"No. I don't think he was mistreated, just. . . ignored. They didn't even know his name, he was just their mother's horse. You'd think they'd take care of him just for that reason, but they couldn't care less."

"Blood is no guarantee."

He said it so flatly it was worse than if he'd been angry, or bitter. Instead, it was as if he was observing that the sky was blue or Texas was big, merely a fact.

She reached out to stroke the horse's neck. "He's not broken, his heart's just broken."

His mouth twisted. "'Just' his heart?"

"The heart is resilient, if you let it be."

He made a sound she couldn't describe, somewhere between a snort and a laugh. A very harsh laugh. A laugh that told her he thought her naïve, or worse.

"I said resilient, not that it couldn't be hurt, and carry scars. Sometimes forever. There are times when I still rage at the world for letting my father die."

He looked at her then, his expression unreadable. "Do you?"

"Yes. Most of the time it's just a sadness that's always there, under the surface. How deep it is depends on how long it's been since something's reminded me. But sometimes it just bubbles up and overflows."

"And what do you do, those times?"

She gave a one-shouldered shrug. "I allow myself the meltdown, as soon as I can. Then I go on. As he would want me to."

"But it doesn't change."

"No." She eyed him for a moment, then decided to risk it while he was apparently willing to talk. "Should it? I loved him so much, it shouldn't fade away, should it?"

His voice went flat. "I don't know. I've never—"

He cut himself off, his jaw tightening as he looked away. Never what, she wondered? Never thought about it? Never felt that way? Never loved anyone like that?

"I'm sorry."

"For what?" He almost snapped it out.

"That you've never."

His gaze snapped back to her face. "I'm not one of your rescues."

"No, you're not. Their minds don't even hold the concept of betrayal."

His brows lowered. "Betrayal?"

"They just know life is miserable. Not that they're being mistreated, by the ones who should be caring for them."

He went very still, and she knew she'd gone that step too far.

"You don't know a damned thing about it."

"No," she admitted easily. "My father might be gone, but while he was here, he loved me as much as any child has ever been loved." She remembered, all too well, what he'd said about his own father. "And I know he didn't want to leave me. It wasn't his choice, not like yours."

He gave that snorting laugh again. "Mine just didn't want to commit murder."

She blinked. "What?"

"He said he had to leave, or he'd kill her."

He looked at her as if he expected her to be shocked. And she was. But she couldn't help asking, "If she was that bad, why didn't he take you with him?"

For a fraction of a second, something flashed in his eyes, across his face, and she knew on some deep, gut level that she'd hit the rawest nerve in him. That she'd hit on the question he'd never been able to answer himself.

He said nothing. Pointedly. Turned his back on her. But she noticed he gave the horse a final pat before he walked to the corral fence. He went over it with a relative ease that told her his ankle was indeed better, and headed toward the gate to his own place. Or rather, she reminded herself, the other part of his place. Because this was his place now, too. And she'd just managed to make her new landlord mad. Again.

She watched him go. He never looked back.

Sighing, she set about caring for the new arrival, who had lapsed back into listlessness. But this time he had food in his belly and had had a gentle touch. He was on the road back, although he didn't know it yet.

Declan Kilcoyne, she wasn't so sure about.

KELSEY RAN A mental total of the donations in her head as she walked along the town square. It wasn't as huge an issue now, thanks to her new landlord, but the donation jars that the various businesses in town kept for the rescue did help a bit, and every flake of hay counted. If the jar in Whiskey River Books held another ten dollars, she'd have enough for another bale, which would feed all the horses for a day. She considered it the town's contribution, and was thankful for all the people, some she knew and some she never would, who tossed their change into the slot in the lid.

She was so used to worrying about such things that it only belatedly hit her that she didn't have to worry about hay for the foreseeable future. Assuming the promised delivery happened, the horses would be set for weeks. Thanks to that guy.

A peal of happy laughter, which echoed her inward emotions at that moment, drew her gaze and she saw two children splashing in the fountain at the foot of Booze Kelly's statue. She wondered, as she often had, what the old cowboy and booze runner would think of it. The rest of the world might chuckle at having a saloon keeper and whiskey runner immortalized in the town square, but this was Whiskey River and they would quickly set those misguided folks right.

A discreet chime rang when she opened the bookshop door. The woman sitting on a stool behind the counter, a book open in her lap looked up as she came in. Melissa Gardiner smiled when she saw her.

"Kelsey! I've been waiting for you."

"Hi, Mel." The woman was relatively new in Whiskey River, having taken over managing the store several months ago. But she had immediately made clear the donation jar would stay; she believed in anything local. And Kelsey knew it was a tough business now, selling actual, physical books. The emptiness of the store now was more proof of that; she was the only one here and she wasn't a customer.

But she could be, now, she realized suddenly.

"Well, that's a happy smile," Mel said with a laugh.

"I just realized that. . . I might actually be able to buy a book now and then."

"I heard things had changed," Mel said tactfully. "I'm happy for you, and your horses."

"Me, too," Kelsey said, meaning it, now that it was finally truly sinking in. "What are you reading?"

"My hottest property," she said, lifting the book so Kelsey could see the cover, which was the same as the display in the window. "Although I think every kid who wanted it was here the night it came out."

"Night?"

"Midnight, on the dot, was when the embargo was lifted. Biggest line I've ever seen, all the way around the square. And they were so excited. I wouldn't have been surprised if some of them had tried to sneak into my storeroom to grab an early copy. Not that I would have cared. I swear, Sam Smith is keeping us in business. They all want the hardcover copies."

Kelsey blinked. Of course she'd noticed the huge displays every time the newest book in the series came out, but she hadn't realized it was quite that big a deal.

"Not to mention," Mel added, "keeping the bugs-as-food businesses going."

She drew back slightly. "Bugs?"

Mel laughed. "From the books. You see, Sam had to live on them for a while, and most kids have never tried them."

"Understandably," Kelsey said, wrinkling her nose.

"I try to get some samples in for the book release parties. The kids try them, but I haven't worked up the nerve myself. Not even the chocolate covered ones."

"Not enough chocolate in the world," Kelsey said. She

looked again at the book. "So, you're reading it so you know all this stuff?"

"Only partly. They're really good," Mel said. "There's a whole second layer there, a bigger, deeper theme, and it's brilliantly done. I know a lot of teachers and counselors have used the books to get through to at risk kids. And I have a lot of adult customers for them, although they tend to leave the midnight rush to the kids."

"And the bugs."

"That too," Mel agreed with a chuckle. "But if you're looking to buy a book, you might want to try the first one." She gestured toward a small stack of books atop the display case. "Declan Bolt is really building a remarkable thing here."

Declan? The titles on the books were in such a large, dramatic font the author name hadn't really registered. Or maybe it just hadn't meant anything to her, until now. But it was an unusual enough name that she reached for the book Mel had indicated. The words "A Sam Smith Adventure" sat above the words "The Escape."

"What does he escape?" she asked.

"Ugliness," Mel said frankly. "That's the deeper level part. Most kids just read it as he had really mean parents, but for adults who know the signs, it was much worse than just mean. There's even a hint in there that they chained him to the wall."

Kelsey's gaze shot to Mel's face. The woman looked immediately apologetic. "Not a spoiler, really, if you want to read it. That's early on. And I don't mean to imply they're grim, they're not. Sam gets into all kinds of scrapes, but he gets himself out by his own wits, and usually helps somebody else in the process."

Kelsey looked at the stacks of books. The pile next to the one she held was titled *On the Run*, and then came *Close Call*. The one Mel was reading, apparently the new one of the four, was rather ominously titled, *Trust No One*.

She flipped to the back of the first book, to the dust jacket flap. The author biography there was beyond brief, and entirely unhelpful.

"Declan Bolt was born in a big city but escaped as soon as he could. He's been moving from place to place ever since, having his own adventures, settling only long enough to write the next Sam Smith story."

There was no author photo.

"Enigmatic," Kelsey murmured.

"Oh, he's way beyond that," Mel said. "I wanted to try and get him for a book signing. I know we're too small for his level, but I wanted to link up with the stores in Fredericksburg and Kerrville, but his publisher says he never, ever does them. Or any other publicity. That's why there's no photograph."

Reclusive. Enigmatic. Horrible parents.

Declan.

"I'll take it," she said impulsively.

Mel grinned. "The mysterious writer thing really intrigues, doesn't it? Do you want me to take that out of the donation money? There's quite a bit this month, thanks to Mr. Bolt."

Kelsey shook her head. "No, this is personal. That's for the horses."

"And that," Mel said with a smile as she rang up the book, "is why people happily donate. They know that with you, the money will go where they want it to."

As she drove home, Kelsey told herself she was being ridiculous. Yes, Declan was not a common name, but the rest was just. . . coincidence, surely? Yet something else niggled at her, a flitting, uncooperative something she couldn't pin down.

She had just made the turn toward the trailer when it finally surfaced.

You're obviously on the verge of bolting. . .

Bolting? The way he'd looked at her. Almost accusingly. *You know.*

Declan Bolt.

She ignored the workers except to give them a brief wave, and hurried inside. She dumped her purse and silenced her phone. She grabbed a Coke, popped the can, and sat down on the couch. For a long moment she simply looked at the book. Finally, she opened it, turned to the title page that mirrored the cover. The next page was a short dedication. *To Frank, for never giving up on me.*

She wondered for a moment who Frank was. A writing teacher, maybe? Agent? Or something more personal. Whoever it was, the words made her question that jump she'd made. Because Declan Kilcoyne didn't seem like he'd be grateful to anyone, or even allow anyone close enough to merit those words.

She briefly pondered running an internet search on both the author and the man acknowledged, but somehow using the internet his generosity—despite his insistence that it was the trust—provided her to snoop on him seemed wrong. Then again, the only thing she'd find would be out there anyway. And it was likely there was no connection, other than the name. The main character's history was, after all, fiction. Wasn't it?

She turned the page. And began to read.

Chapter Seventeen

THIS HAD ALL been a big mistake.

Getting off the hamster wheel his life had become.

Thinking it was time to settle in one place.

Thinking that one place could be in the state he'd been born in, even if it was hundreds of miles from where he'd started.

It had all been a mistake, possibly the biggest of a life full of them.

He'd been holed up in the office for three days, barely remembering to eat, staring endlessly at a screen on which a cursor blinked unrelentingly on a blank page. On some level, he knew he was he was falling into old pathways he'd thought long beaten, but he couldn't seem to stop.

Before, when he'd started to feel this way he would dive into Sam's life, because in that world he could fix things. But now, even Sam, so much cleverer and braver than Declan, was trapped and there was no way out. And that damned cursor blinked on.

He knew how desperate he had gotten when he realized

he was wishing he could call Frank. But Frank was dead, and never again would he be able to turn to the man who had been one source of sanity in his insane life.

Another run, he thought. But he'd already done two circuits of the boundary today, another would likely make his ankle flare up again. A swim then. That helped sometimes if he was stuck. But he'd done that today, too, and it had resulted in nothing except making him clean since he'd had to rinse off after. And he was weary enough he might just end up drowning and, as bad as he felt, that particular desire had been beaten well back into its cage.

Food. Maybe he should eat something. *Didn't they say you had to feed your brain if nothing else?* But that meant leaving the office and going down to the kitchen. Leaving the office with Sam's problem still unsolved, the cursor still blinking on that blank page.

Definitely hamster wheel. And about as useful.

He shoved back his chair and stood. This was pointless. Maybe he should be spending this energy figuring out what he was going to do now that he apparently wasn't a writer anymore.

He headed downstairs, to the kitchen. The room was nothing if not eclectic, dramatically grained hickory cabinets, a greenish granite countertop, rough stone walls and gleaming stainless steel. It was a bit overpowering, but fit his mood right now.

He opened the freezer. Stood there staring at the labels

on the various meals Zee had neatly stacked. Nothing appealed despite the variety. He dug into the meat drawer. Found a thick steak that looked tempting. Realized it was so thick it would take hours to thaw. He'd tried doing it in the microwave once, but it had ended up cooking the outside and leaving the inside frozen; it was clearly a knack he didn't have.

He stood there, staring at the steak as his fingers grew numb from holding the froze chunk of beef. And finally admitted what he wanted wasn't the steak. He wanted the feeling he'd had the last time he'd had a steak.

With Kelsey.

He groaned aloud. Threw the steak back in the drawer. Slammed the freezer door shut. To hell with it. He wasn't really hungry anyway, it had just been something to accomplish when he couldn't seem to do anything else.

He heard the faint sound of knocking on the front door. Glanced at the clock on the oven; it was nearly seven. Business day was over. No one was due. He didn't need a calendar to check, he allowed too few people to invade his world to need help tracking them. Speaking of which, how had they gotten through the gate? And he hadn't heard a car, either.

There was only one obvious answer. The one person who didn't use the main gate, and who often didn't drive but rode.

Kelsey.

He couldn't. She tangled him up too much, and he was already in knots. She made him wish for things he could never have, and he didn't need that frustration piled on top of what he was already feeling.

He ignored the sound. Opened the refrigerator in search of something quick and fast he could take back to the office. Found some apples in the crisper, and some lunch meat in the deli drawer. Grabbed one of the apples and yanked a few thin slices of the smoked chicken out of the package. He ate the meat as he stood there, barely tasting it. It would be enough, with the apple. He closed the refrigerator door. He'd go back to the tower, and he wouldn't leave the damned office until—

He froze in the act of turning. Stared at the figure on the patio, between the wall of windows and the pool.

Kelsey.

His heart slammed in his chest. He wanted to look away, pretend he hadn't seen her, but he couldn't. Then he wondered if she was really there, or if had he conjured her up out of an imagination that had run dry everywhere else.

He was there, had his hand on the handle of the sliding glass door, before he was even consciously aware of having decided to do it. Interesting, he noted rather numbly, that he was apparently incapable of doing what he did most times, which was turn his back on intruders. He needed a freaking butler. No, that would just be someone else to deal with. Maybe a droid butler. That would work. He'd have to look into investing in some clever robotics firm.

He'd meant to just find out why she was here, not to invite her in, but she didn't give him the chance. She stepped inside. Said nothing, just looked at him. He wondered if she could hear his heartbeat; it seemed so loud to him he couldn't see how she could not. He felt the craziest urge to lean in and kiss her. His pulse went even wilder at the thought, and his entire body tightened in an anticipation that took his breath away. What the hell?

Belatedly, he realized that giving in to that urge could well solve his problem, because she'd probably take off running. After trying—and quite possibly succeeding; he'd seen how strong she was—to punch his lights out.

"Can we sit down for a moment? There's something I'd like to ask you."

He was reeling a bit, it had been a very long time since he'd felt anything like this. Otherwise, he might have turned her away, or at least asked what made her think he would answer whatever she wanted to ask in the first place. But instead he found himself standing aside, letting her walk into the living room. He saw her glance around at the somewhat minimalist furnishings, a curved, soft leather couch facing an entertainment center, a couple of tables, chairs, and rugs. Saw her look down at the polished wood floor and up to the open wood trusses of the vaulted ceiling and the big ceiling fan.

He'd never really thought about what the place would

look like to others, because he never planned on having anyone in here. He had a room with a separate entrance on the bottom floor of the tower where he usually met with anyone he was forced to deal with face to face. Few were allowed into the rest of his domain, and that was the way he liked it.

And yet here she was. Taking a seat on that couch and looking at him as if she expected him to join her.

He took one of the chairs. Occupying the same piece of furniture she sat on seemed the height of folly at the moment, given the crazy way he was reacting to her.

Tasty.

The word from their earlier exchange crashed into his mind. And again he thought about kissing her, finding out just how tasty she would be.

He gave himself an inward shake.

"You had a question?" he said, his effort to make his voice neutral coming off more as gruff.

And then she blasted every other thought out of his mind.

"Who's Frank?"

Chapter Eighteen

K ELSEY SAW THE shock flash across his face. It was quickly followed by a rather determined impassivity.

"Who?" he said.

She sighed inwardly. She'd known this wasn't going to be easy but hadn't been able to talk herself out of it any more than she'd been able to understand why she felt compelled to do it.

"You know who I mean. Who is he?"

"I don't know—"

She held up a hand, cutting him off. "Please. I'll keep your secret. I don't get why you'd want to hide who you are, but I'm sure you have your reasons"

"Hasn't stopped you from coming over here and prying, though, has it?"

"Raging curiosity," she said, although she knew quite well it was more than that.

"And we all know how that ends," he said, his tone warning.

"I'm not a cat."

"No, you're not. They generally know when they're not wanted."

She studied him silently. She remembered the moment when, about three-quarters of the way through the first book, she'd become certain. She'd finished it late at night and wished she had the next right now. She'd found e-book versions at the library, but there was a long waiting list for all of them. And she didn't want to wait. So she'd splurged and bought the second and downloaded it to her phone. And then the next, and then the current one. And ended up reading until the wee hours, sleeping only when she couldn't keep her eyes open any longer.

Over the next three days she'd gotten a minimal amount of work done as she lived in the fictional world of a young boy named Sam Smith. She was so lost in that world that most of the time she forgot exactly why she had started this, because nothing mattered but finding out what happened next. It was the purest reading experience she'd had in a long time, and only when she finished a book did it come back to her.

And along with remembering why she'd begun, she remembered the clues along the way, like breadcrumbs scattered throughout the stories, a way of speaking here, an attitude there. But most of all it was there in Sam's awful backstory, his history, the abusive home that had been so horrific he'd escaped when he was only twelve and, by his wits, managed to survive.

Always on the move, Sam had gone from place to place, the only constant putting more distance between him and that place where he should have been safe. He rarely trusted, he'd learned those lessons well, but about half the time when he did he was betrayed. At the end of the fourth, newest book, Sam was in such a bad place that her heart ached for him.

"Who's Frank?" she asked again, a question born out of her fear that too much of what haunted Sam was real. She desperately needed to know he'd had someone in his life who had helped.

She'd been bursting with it when she'd turned the last page, and had had to talk to someone. Her dearest confidant was the natural place to turn. She knew her mother would be kindly disposed, not just because it was her nature, but because Declan had helped her daughter.

Those things in the books. . . mom, I think they're so real because he's lived them, or things like them.

Then you have your work cut out for you.

Love had flooded her all over again as her mother not only accepted she was right about Declan Bolt's identity, but that she would continue to try to break through the wall he surrounded himself with.

At her repeated question, Declan stared at her silently.

"I understand." Her voice was quiet, gentle. "Sometimes you need to shut out the world. Sometimes it deserves to be shut out. But you can't live there, behind those walls, forever."

"Says who?" he muttered.

"Says someone who tried." He looked surprised enough that she seized on it and continued. "After dad was killed, I retreated. I hid. I ran away. Whatever I had to do not to deal with the world that had taken him from me. If my mother didn't have the patience of a saint, if she hadn't loved me far too much to let me continue down that path, I could have ended up. . ."

She let her voice trail off, and gestured around her to the house that had become his fortress. He said nothing. But neither did he try again to throw her out. So she kept on.

"And all this amid her own grief, which was so great that she has never seriously looked at another man, in all these years. Instead, once she'd salvaged me, she turned to others. Countless times she helped survivors who were in such pain after their loved one's death that they shut out the world."

"Don't know the feeling." He sounded dismissive of the thought.

She considered that for a moment. "Is that," she asked, her voice quiet and laced with sadness, "because you've never really had a loved one?"

Something flickered in his expression again, and she knew.

"There must have been someone in your life, at least once, who honestly cared about you. Was it Frank?"

"You don't know a—"

"Damn thing about you. Got it. By the way, that was one of the most effective things you did. Having a boy that young say that so often just pounded home how he must have grown up. It was wrenching."

He stared at her again, but this time she saw a trace of something new, something she couldn't quite name, in the tightness of his mouth, and around his eyes. "I think you're confusing me with a fictional character."

"Perhaps because you put so much of yourself into him."

"Kelsey," he said, the sound of her name from him giving her a jolt, a reaction so unwise she groaned inwardly at herself. "Whatever you think you know—"

"The copyright on the books. The Shipley Trust," she said, laying down the trump card, the thing that had merely put the seal on what she already knew. "My new landlord."

His eyes widened, just slightly. And then he closed them as the inevitability of it seemed to descend on him, and his expression showed it, as did the long, weary breath he let out.

"Damn."

"Yes."

"Who the hell reads the copyright page?"

"I did." She knew she had no right to press, didn't know why he hadn't thrown her out yet, but as long as he didn't she wasn't giving up. She'd learned well. And for the fourth time she asked, "Who's Frank?"

His eyes opened. He let out a bewildered sounding half-chuckle. "Out of all this, that's what you care about?"

"It's who you cared about, enough to write that. And apparently the only one, since there are no dedications in the rest."

He blinked. "You read them. . . all?"

Some part of her mind realized he'd given in, that he was no longer denying, but she knew better than to even point it out. She just kept going. As her mother had often said, "You never knew for sure where the weak spot in someone's wall was until you found it and pushed hard enough."

"Yes. I couldn't stop. They're magnificent. And I'll be joining the crowd, anxiously awaiting the next one."

Something new, something she almost thought was fear, flickered in his eyes. And when he spoke, she knew she'd been right, because suddenly the question she'd originally asked now was more palatable than what she'd just said.

"Frank was a cop."

She started to ask if "was" meant he'd retired. . . or died. But some instinct warned her off that and, instead, she asked, "How'd you meet him?"

He gave her a sideways look, but again he didn't end this in any of the several ways he could have, including simply getting up and walking away. Retreating into that rough, stone tower of his, for instance.

"He caught me stealing," he said bluntly.

"Stealing what?"

"Does it matter?"

"It might. What?"

"A carton of milk."

She drew back slightly. That, she hadn't expected. "Why milk?"

"Protein and fluid."

"That's why you took it?"

"I needed both."

Her brow furrowed. "How old were you?"

"Twelve."

It belatedly struck her that him knowing about the content of milk wasn't as odd as a twelve-year-old who stole, not candy or even an apple, but something with protein and fluid.

"Thirsty and hungry?" she asked.

He shrugged. "Seemed smarter to only steal one thing. But I got caught anyway."

"By Frank."

He nodded.

"What did he do with you?"

"After he chewed me out and threatened to drag me to the station and throw me in a cell?"

She could only imagine how terrifying that must have been to such a young boy. Or maybe not, if Sam's story was indeed a version of his own; if so, he'd been through worse much younger.

"Yes, after that."

For the first time, she saw a softness in his expression.

And there it was, the emotion that had inspired the dedication. He picked at a loose thread on the frayed hem of his t-shirt. Now that she knew who he was, the worn clothes seemed . . . important somehow.

"He took me home with him," he finally said. "His wife had died recently, and he had nobody else, so I guess I was a distraction. He fed me dinner. At his own table. Made me go slow, so I wouldn't throw it all back up."

That alone told her volumes about how starved he must have been. And reminded her of how he'd been with a certain starved horse.

"Did you tell him? What was happening?" she asked softly.

"Some. He tried to get me to tell him where I lived. I knew if I told him I'd have to go back."

"I'll bet that jail cell didn't sound so bad then."

His head snapped up. He stared at her. "That's what I told him. That I'd rather he just threw me in that cell."

"What did he say?"

He lowered his gaze again to that loose thread. "He asked what would happen if I went home. I told him. . . she would kill me."

Kelsey's stomach knotted. "And you meant it, literally, didn't you." It wasn't really a question, because she already knew the answer.

"Yes."

"Do you still believe that, now?"

He lifted his gaze to hers then. "Yes," he said, and she'd never seen a more desolate expression. And why not, when you were admitting that your own mother would have murdered you.

She couldn't bear that look in his eyes, and hastily asked, "Where's Frank now?"

His jaw tightened. "Dead."

So in trying to avoid one pain, she'd swerved into another. "I'm sorry. Truly. He was obviously an amazing man."

"Yes."

"When?"

The pain in his expression seemed to ease a bit. "Last year."

Her own distress loosened up a notch. "Then he knew."

For the first time he smiled, barely. "Yes. He saw the first book, with the dedication, hit print. And then some best seller lists. And he saw it. . . take off, the whole thing."

"The Sam Smith phenomenon, the kids lined up at bookstores, the themed parties, the cosplay, the screens around the world lit up with your words?"

He let out an audible breath. "Yes. All that."

"Thank goodness."

"Yes. I'll be eternally grateful for that."

"One thing, at least."

"Yes."

"I'm glad."

His gaze locked on her face. She said nothing, just held

her eyes steady.

"I believe you," he said after a long, silent moment.

And Kelsey thought she'd witnessed a bit of a miracle in those three words from this man. And that was more progress than she'd ever expected in one evening.

"What happened, after he caught you?"

"He went and talked to her. Went all bad cop on her. Told her he would be meeting me every day, and if he saw so much as a bruise he was coming after her."

Kelsey wanted to cheer. As it was a wide grin spread across her face. "I hoped that stopped her."

"In a way."

"What way?"

"She didn't hit me anymore. But it brought the emotional torture to a higher level." He tugged at that thread, and at last it broke. He held it up, studied it as if it held the answer to the universe. At that moment, perhaps that thread that had finally broken free did hold the answer to his.

"Did Frank know?"

He nodded, still looking at the thread. "He spent about an hour almost every day counteracting it. Telling me I wasn't worthless and stupid, I was smarter than her, smarter than him even, smart enough not to believe her crap. And every weekend I went to his house. He made her let me. He fed me, talked to me, taught me."

"Above and beyond the call of duty," Kelsey whispered.

He looked at her then. "Yes. Way above. If it wasn't for

Frank, I'd be dead, one way or another. And then, on my birthday, he gave me a journal. Told me to tell it everything when I couldn't talk to him."

And a writer was born. . .

"Do you still have it?"

Again he looked surprised, as if he hadn't expected that question. But he nodded. "I had to hide it from her, she would have tossed it and me into a shredder if she'd found it."

She wondered, briefly, what his mother's own past had been like, to make her what she was, but nothing excused what she'd done.

"Well, when you finally have kids, you'll have the perfect bad example not to follow."

His eyes widened at her first words. "That," he said flatly, "will never happen. You think I'd risk that?"

"You wouldn't be like her. And you get kids. That's obvious from Sam."

His jaw tightened, and she knew he wasn't going to be moved on that. At least, not now. And she wasn't sure she could blame him.

"I want you to meet my mother, some day," she said.

His brow furrowed at the seeming non sequitur. He looked away. Said nothing.

"You do know they're not all like yours, right?"

He gave a half-shrug she took to mean he did know, but it made little difference to him. She could understand that.

His silence, his avoiding her gaze, told her she'd pushed as far as she could on this.

"I'll keep your secret, you know. No one will find out from me."

"If anyone does, I'll know who to thank," he said, his tone sharper now.

"I'm sorry Frank's gone. But he must have been very proud."

"He was." It was almost a whisper. "And I was able to take care of him, at the end."

Something hit her then. "What was Frank's last name?"

He looked at her then. For a moment she thought he wouldn't answer. But then he did. "Shipley."

"The Shipley Trust," she whispered. "It was for him, wasn't it? To take care of him."

"In case anything happened to me. And then. . . I kept the name."

"As tribute," she said.

He nodded, and fell silent.

It was amazing he'd talked as much as he had. Perhaps it had simply been bottled up too long, and she'd asked the right thing at the right time. But it was clear he was done, and she accepted it. And changed the subject completely.

"So what's next for the intrepid Sam?"

That suddenly it all vanished. The softening, the openness, were gone as abruptly as if he'd slammed a door. He didn't stand up so much as erupt onto his feet.

"Nothing," he said, his voice harsh.

"What?"

"Sam Smith is dead."

He did then what she'd half-expected from the moment he'd let her in. He turned on his heel and walked out.

Chapter Nineteen

THE MOMENT HE stepped into his office and the door closed behind him, he sagged against it and slid to the floor. He'd skipped the elevator and used the stairs, running up both flights to the third level of the tower.

He felt utterly drained. And strangely detached. As if it had been someone else spilling his guts out onto the floor down there. And yet as if telling the grim tale had opened a spigot and emptied every last bit of life out of him.

You need to confront it. Admit it. Own it. That's the only way that it won't own you for the rest of your life.

Frank's wise words drifted through a mind too weary now to latch onto them. But he'd confronted it all right. And left the person who had pushed him to it downstairs in his house. Inside the fortress walls.

He'd wanted that fortress. He'd needed at least the illusion of security. And after several years of moving around, he'd wanted to test if he could stay in one place and still function. And he had, until a few months ago. The time here had been just what he'd hoped for. He'd been productive, and finally able to say with honesty that in some ways he didn't regret his turbulent childhood, because it was the driving force behind his success.

He'd been both surprised and pleased by how well he'd settled in. Until that little bastard Sam had decided to stay in the damned hole he'd written him into.

And Kelsey Blaine had barreled into his life.

He thought of that old saying that no good deed goes unpunished. Well, if helping out the Whiskey River Rescue had been a good deed, he sure was reaping the punishment for it.

Except that looking at Kelsey Blaine could hardly be classified as punishment. Not to any man breathing, anyway. He closed his eyes as if she were still there before him.

Talking to her, on the other hand, had seemed beyond him. Until tonight, when he couldn't seem to shut up. When he'd poured the whole ugly mess out in front of her. He couldn't believe he'd really done that. He'd never told anyone except Frank what he'd told her tonight. Although, like Frank, she seemed to guess even at what he hadn't said.

He realized then, still in that odd, detached way, that she had the same sort of intuitive understanding Frank had had. Frank had lost the wife he'd loved. Kelsey had lost the father she adored. Connection?

As if the effort of that thought had sapped the last little bit of his brainpower, he felt a wave of dizzying exhaustion sweep over him.

He awoke on the couch against the office wall, with no memory of getting there. It wasn't the first time it had happened. It was there for the times when, on a tight deadline, he'd holed up to write for long hours.

Never a tighter deadline than now.

And yet he still had no answer.

"I've got an answer all right," he muttered aloud. "There is no way out. Sam's done."

Saying it, speaking it to her had given him a bleak feeling he hadn't felt since he'd begun to write the tales of. . . what had Kelsey called him? The intrepid Sam?

Kelsey.

He'd crashed hard, slept for nearly four hours. He wondered how long she had stayed after he'd bailed. Wondered if that curiosity of hers had led her to snoop. He didn't really care. There was little of him in that part of the house. A book on the end table, a statement from the trust, and maybe his watch list queue if she really started poking around. The alarm system, likely unnecessary as isolated as he was, might hint he was a bit paranoid about privacy, but then she already knew that. No, she wouldn't find many answers down there.

Because they were all up here.

It was all here, from that first, now battered journal to that set of x-rays of his ankle, to the only photograph he had of himself as a child, taken by Frank as he opened the gift of that journal, the gift that had changed him forever.

No, he amended silently as he looked at the image that hung on the stone wall behind his desk, it was Frank himself who had changed Declan forever. Had saved him, when he didn't think himself worth saving.

And now he couldn't even save a fictional boy. It was hopeless, and he was well into feeling that way.

He never even turned on the computer. Instead he went back downstairs, every step of the way insisting that he wasn't hoping that she'd stayed. Why would she? And he didn't want to face her again, did he? Of course not, that would be crazy.

Crazy Joe.

Suddenly the moniker seemed entirely appropriate.

The living room was empty. The room he'd always liked because of the spaciousness the vaulted ceilings gave it now seemed cold, echoing his footsteps over the wood floor in a way that he'd never noticed before. A sad sort of sound. A lonely sound.

Oh, yeah, Crazy Joe. Completely cray-cray.

He stopped, listening. There wasn't a sound to be heard, not from this room, or the kitchen, or even outside. He walked over to the couch, sat down where she had been. As expected, there was no lingering trace of her warmth on the cool leather.

Only then did he notice the piece of paper on the low table in front of the couch. He stared at it for a moment, seeing the lines of handwriting on it, knowing it had to be hers. It took him far too long to finally reach out and pick it up. It was dog-eared, and had been folded, as if she'd had it tucked away somewhere. But he barely noticed that as he read.

Declan—

I've added admiration to the list of things I feel about you. You've taken a hideous past and turned it into a way to reach millions of kids around the world, some of whom might well be living a life like your own. You give them the escape you never had, and that's an amazing, wonderful thing.

Thank you.

Kelsey

The sentiment of the note wasn't new, adult readers, his editors, and reviewers had all said similar things. But the way she put it seemed to mean more. To him, at least.

But that might be because of the way his eyes first snagged, and then kept going back to that first sentence.

. . .the list of things I feel about you.

And he was seized with the need to know what those other things were. If any of them were anything close to what he was feeling about her. And no amount of ordering himself to back off, to be glad she was gone and he had his solitude back, seemed to ease that need.

Thank you.

For what? Pouring out the battery acid that was his past?

Did women really value that kind of torturous soul-baring that much?

He held the note, staring at it, for a long time. He practically had it memorized by the time he realized it had been written on the back of something. He turned the paper over. It was a form letter making an annual request that she verify her contact information had not changed, for the records of an investment company in California. Her father's insurance, he guessed.

He was about to turn it back and read the note yet again when a series of numbers caught his eye.

Her phone number.

He could have gotten it anyway, from the trust records, or the investigation report. But somehow this seemed different. Because she'd left it here? Or was he simply interested now, where he hadn't been before? And, in the end, what difference did it really make? He had the number, a way of reaching her that didn't require him to show up at her place in person. That was good, wasn't it?

Except he hadn't minded the evening he'd spent there. At all.

A sudden visual popped into his writer's head, of an invasive vine slowly but inexorably wrapping itself around a tree, eventually smothering it. Connections, he thought again. That was what they'd always been to him, invasive. And betraying, in the end. What seemed harmless, friendly, trustworthy in the beginning always ended up the opposite.

Frank had told him that when he was older he would have learned enough to judge who was trustworthy and who wasn't, but secretly he'd always thought it safer to trust no one. Eventually he'd let a very few in. True Mahan. David, his agent of five years now. And Marcus, the lawyer he'd found through of all things, his son's fan letter, and who oversaw the hands-on work of the trust.

The trust that had, in the end, betrayed him to her. He was buried deep enough in the paperwork that only those who had to knew he was connected to the trust. It should have stayed that way, but somehow she'd found out.

And he had never expected anyone who knew he was connected to the trust to read not just the books but the copyright page. Most of his target readers didn't even know what the copyright page was, except that thing with the tiny print they had to skip past to get to the story. And anyone who did wouldn't have the piece Kelsey had, that he—Crazy Joe Kilcoyne—was the Shipley Trust.

He sat there, thinking, his mind darting from pillar to post. He could text her now that he had the number at hand. But he didn't want to. He wanted to find out if she was asleep, and hear what she sounded like if she had been. And after that it became a fight against the urge to pick up his phone and dial that number.

Which was the most ridiculous urge he'd had in his life.

He sat there holding the note, and staring down his phone, until the first light of dawn streaked the sky.

Chapter Twenty

KELSEY WAS DRYING her hair, still enjoying the novelty of being able to do it without tripping the circuit breaker on the cabin's old, tired wiring, when she thought she heard something. She turned off the dryer and listened for a moment until she heard the ring of her cell. It wasn't her mother's melodic tone, which was an instant relief; it was five AM in California, and those calls were never good. It was instead the ring assigned to callers outside her contact list. It was probably a spam call, but she walked out into the living area to check.

She didn't recognize the number, but the name assigned to it kick-started her pulse. *Shipley Trust.*

Declan.

She'd lain awake for a long time, replaying last night in her head. She'd been as amazed that he'd told her as she'd been at the story itself. And more awed overall at what he'd overcome to accomplish what he had. Which was why she'd felt compelled to leave that note for him.

She took in a deep breath, and picked up the phone.

"Hello?"

Silence.

"Declan?"

More silence. Regretting he'd called?

"Are you there?"

"Yes."

She let out the breath at last. When he said nothing more, she started to get concerned. "Are you all right?"

She heard a low sound that could have been a wry chuckle. "For a guy who went completely off the rails last night, you mean?"

"No. For a guy who let out a lot of pain he should never have had to carry."

"Feeling sorry for me?"

"Is that what you want?"

"No."

She hadn't thought so, but it was good to hear him say it.

"I saw your light on, so I knew you were awake," he said, and it took her a moment to realize he was explaining the 7AM call.

I didn't sleep much.

That was something she didn't want to say, and she scrambled for something else. "How about breakfast?"

"What?"

"I have to feed the horses first, but then I was looking for an excuse to make my favorite apple pancake, and it's too big for just me."

Again there was silence, and then, "How's the new arrival?"

"Oliver? He's already doing better," she said, figuring this was his way of saying no to the invitation. It had been an impulse thing anyway, so she wasn't surprised.

"Oliver?"

"Like in *Oliver Twist.*"

"As in 'please, sir, I want some more,'?"

"Exactly."

He chuckled. It was short, and quiet, but she'd take it. And kept talking, finding the fact that he was still talking at all rather flattering.

I've never seen him unsettled by anyone. Except you.

True Mahan's words came back to her. That had flattered her, too. And she should spend a bit more time analyzing her fascination with this man, which had begun long before she'd found out his secret. In fact, had begun the first moment she'd laid eyes on him, when she'd thought him Crazy Joe's gardener.

"Kelsey?"

Glad he wasn't here to see her blush, she went on quickly. "He's not gobbling, so I think he's starting to realize there will be food for him. And he's showing some interest in the rest of the crew, which he didn't have the energy for when he got here."

"I'm glad."

"Me, too. He's really quite sweet. Very nice temperament, considering."

Another moment of silence. Which made his next words surprising.

"What time?"

"Time?"

"Breakfast."

She found herself smiling as she answered, "Come any time. If I'm not at the trailer I'll be out with the horses."

She quickly finished drying her hair, and was halfway through applying mascara before she realized she was actually putting on makeup. For a day she'd planned on spending working with Oliver. Yes, it was past time to figure out exactly how she felt about Declan Kilcoyne.

She hastily double-checked that she had what she needed for breakfast, then headed quickly out to the corral. She could see even from here that Oliver was standing at the fence where the other horses were gathered. They appeared to be getting along fine, socializing in the way horses did, and she had hopes that as soon as he was a little steadier, and didn't need such careful feeding and monitoring, she could move him into the main corral with them. Horses were herd animals, and she thought he'd be happier there, but he had to be able to hold his own before it would be safe for him.

Oliver had just finished the small amount of sweet feed Dr. Barrett had recommended for the first couple of weeks when his head came up and he nickered softly. Kelsey guessed before she looked.

"He remembers you," she said as Declan reached the corral fence and Oliver ambled over to greet him. "And fondly," she added as the horse gently nudged him with his nose.

She was pleased, both by the horse's growing confidence and the slight smile on Declan's face as he rubbed that spot under Oliver's jaw. She'd be able to remove the halter she always left on newcomers for the first couple of weeks soon, he was acclimating so fast.

"You walked?" she asked, not having heard a vehicle. He nodded. "You need a horse."

He looked at her over Oliver's withers. "You think everyone needs a horse."

"True. But you especially."

"Why me especially?"

"To give you something outside yourself to worry about."

His brows lowered. "Saying I'm self-centered?"

"With your life, it would be a miracle if you weren't. I'm just saying having a horse to take care of might help. With many things."

"So now you're saying I need a lot of help?"

"I didn't say that." This was not going well, she thought. "I wouldn't presume to tell you that."

"But you think so."

She eyed him narrowly. "Did you come over here spoiling for a fight?"

He just looked at her for a moment, then, with the barest trace of amusement he said, "Maybe."

She hadn't expected that, and nearly smiled.

"Or maybe I just wanted to see what it would take to get you to fight."

"Oh, that's easy. Hurt one of them," she said waving at her small herd. "But you've already seen me fighting mad."

"That was before you knew."

"Knew?" She wondered if he expected some kind of special dispensation because of who he was. Supposed he got it, from most. She herself had to admit she was a bit in awe of what he did, especially after reading the books straight through.

"That I was the Shipley Trust."

She blinked. In the astonishment of discovering he was the most popular new kid's author of this decade, the fact that he was also her landlord had gotten pushed into the background.

"Oh. Testing to see if I'd risk making my landlord mad?"

"Maybe more testing to see if that's all I am."

She fought not to read more into those words than were there. He hadn't asked if that's all he was to her specifically. "You are," she said carefully, "much more than that."

She was about to add "To a lot of people," to that, but something about the way his expression lightened, with a flicker of something that almost looked like relief crossing his face, stopped her.

The horses seen to, they went back to the trailer. She washed her hands and set the oven to preheat, then gathered ingredients.

"Can I do something?" he asked politely.

"Are you any good at peeling apples?"

"How hard can it be?"

"Ask again when you're bleeding," she said dryly, handing him a paring knife and the half-dozen apples she'd set aside. He gave her a sideways look, but once more she saw the trace of a smile at the corners of his mouth. It warmed her far too much for such a small expression.

She set about putting together the rest of the ingredients, including the vanilla she'd picked up yesterday.

"It's nice to be able to do this again, in a real kitchen, with real tools," she said when the batter was ready. "Like actual measuring spoons."

He looked up from where he was doing a rather too careful job of piling up apple peelings. "You have everything you need?"

"More than I'll use," she said. "Thank you." She set about slicing his decently peeled apples into wedges.

"That wasn't fishing for a thank-you."

"You don't have to fish. I am beyond thankful."

"I just wanted you to be able to focus on the horses, not on wondering if your roof was going to fall in on you."

"There were moments," she said with a wry smile. "But I was glad I even had a roof."

He was silent for a moment as she arranged the last apple, poured in the batter. Then, without looking at her, he asked, "How is Mr. Roper?"

That surprised her. "He's doing much better." She hesitated, then added, "It helps that his money worries are over. Since you paid him three times what this land is worth."

He shrugged, not looking at her. "Trust decision."

"Um-hmm. Like this was?" She slid the pan into the oven, then gestured around her shiny new kitchen.

He shrugged again.

"Tell me something," she said conversationally, "were you behind that big donation to the rescue last year?"

He gave her a startled look then, and she knew her guess had been right.

"Why is it so hard to accept thanks for your generosity?" she asked.

"Because I know how hard it is to feel like you owe somebody. It's easier if it's some faceless entity, some thing, not someone."

She studied him for a moment. "Frank?"

He stared at the pile of apple peelings. "No matter what I did, it could never be enough."

She thought about her next words carefully. "From a step back, and from what you told me about him, I can assure you, Declan Bolt, that seeing your success, seeing what you did for other kids, was more than enough. And that's not even counting what you've done with your success."

He turned then. She looked up at him, wishing she could find the words to help, but her own experience was so vastly different she had no idea where to even start. Yes, she'd lost her wonderful father, but at least she'd had him. And her amazing mother. Where he'd had—

He moved so quickly she didn't have time to react before his mouth was on hers. The kiss was urgent, almost fierce at first, and she was so startled it took a moment for her to realize it had gentled. And a moment longer to recognize the warmth spreading through her was starting there, at her lips, where he was tasting her.

Only when he broke the kiss, jerking back in a way that looked almost involuntary, did she truly feel it the force of it, by the way she regretted that he'd stopped. She stared at him, stunned both that he'd done it, and her own response.

Slowly, she realized he looked as stunned as she felt.

"I didn't—I shouldn't—"

"Don't ruin it by apologizing," she said, finding her voice in time to cut off his stammered words.

He fell silent. And looked as if he wanted more than anything to retreat to his fortress.

She put him to setting the table before he could.

Chapter Twenty-One

DON'T RUIN IT.

Her words echoed in his head. It had to be something good, didn't it, if she didn't want it ruined? If it had sucked, she wouldn't care, right? And if she didn't want it ruined, then she didn't mind him doing it?

He nearly groaned aloud as he lined up the utensils perfectly on the table, not because he was obsessive about it but because he needed something else to do, to focus on. He hadn't spent so much effort analyzing three little words since the first sentence of the first book.

Well, and the three next words on the current book, those words that simply wouldn't come.

And that that had popped up told him how desperate he was, that even his current writing dilemma was preferable to thinking about what had just happened. And telling himself it was just a kiss wasn't working worth a damn.

Because it had been much, much more. And deep in his gut he knew it wasn't simply because it had been the first time in years he'd kissed a woman simply because he wanted to, and not because it was a time-limited hookup that would be forgotten as soon as it was over. Or because he'd given up on those soulless encounters so long ago he'd begun to think himself as successfully disinterested in the whole process.

Shit. Shit, shit, *shit.*

He should have known. Should have known the day she came barreling up to confront Crazy Joe that she was going to be trouble.

He'd just never expected her to be this kind of trouble.

Only his long ago vow that he would never again run in fear kept him from doing just that. It wasn't that kind of fear anyway. Not that he liked this feeling any better.

But he'd liked that kiss.

He nearly laughed at himself. Liked it? He'd practically spontaneously combusted.

"How do you feel about bacon?"

The mundane inquiry yanked him out of thoughts best left behind anyway.

"Um. . . sixth food group?"

She grinned. "Man after my own heart. Lots of bacon it is."

He'd never really thought about that phrase before. Wondered how it had gone from the literal meaning of the words to merely indicating a sharing of taste or outlook rather than. . . well, the literal meaning. *After my own heart. . .* Literally, it could be rather grim. Serial killer stuff. Figuratively, it could be. . . many things. Never having been after anyone's heart, he wasn't sure—

Stop it.

Recognition of what he was doing, focusing on such things, just like he did when he hit a writing speed bump— or in this case roadblock, complete with barricades and flashing lights—had him feeling pretty grim when breakfast hit the table. But when he bit into the pancake, a baked affair, thick with the apples he'd peeled, everything vanished except the sweet, rich, luscious taste.

"Wow," he said, looking across the gleaming table at her.

She grinned. "Good, isn't it?"

"Amazing. It's like apple pie for breakfast."

"But much less decadent," she said, "because it's just a pancake. What's in a name, huh?"

He couldn't help himself, he smiled back at her. "I thought you said you weren't a cook."

She gestured at the pan on the hot pad, sitting there inviting a grab for a second helping. "Baking," she said. "Entirely different thing."

His brow furrowed.

"Baking is almost chemistry. Proportions, timing, temperature, all that. Cooking is. . . art. At least the way my mother does it."

"Doesn't she expect you to do it the same?"

"Mom?" She laughed. "She gave up on that early on. I know the basics, so I won't starve, but she says I should visit more often to get some real food."

"Do you?"

"Haven't for a while, but that's because she came here when I broke my arm last year." She laughed again.

She did it a lot, and easily. Even though the thought of her with a broken bone made him wince inwardly.

"How did that happen?"

Her expression went sad for a moment. "Tough old dun gelding who was too far gone to help."

So she did lose some. He'd wondered, but hadn't wanted to ask. Whether it was because he would be expected to share in return or simply that he didn't want to make her think about it, he wasn't sure.

"Anyway, Mom had a fit when she saw the cabin. A hot plate and an old toaster oven are not her idea of a functional kitchen. She rented an apartment for a month and moved us in."

He blinked. "She what?"

"I swear, all she did was cook for me. Well, and took care of the horses."

He drew back then. "Your mother took care of the rescue horses?"

Kelsey nodded. "So I didn't have to with my arm. Did a fine job, too. It's not her passion, but she gets it."

He felt strangely off balance. He'd never pictured, even with Frank, that kind of relationship. He didn't know enough to even imagine. Didn't know what to think. He took refuge in going for that second helping he wanted anyway. She looked pleased. Which oddly, pleased him.

This whole thing was confusing. He wasn't sure if he'd made the best decision in coming here, or the worst mistake of his life.

"Will you get mad at me and walk out if I ask you something?"

That quickly all the defenses snapped back into place. "That depends," he said guardedly.

"I won't ask what's next, but. . . you didn't really mean Sam is dead, did you?"

He'd been afraid that was where she was going.

"He might as well be."

He took a bite almost angrily, the sweet of the pancake and the tart of the apple now seeming to hit all the wrong notes in his mouth. This was what he'd been afraid of, that because she had shared so much of her own story that she would expect him to do the same. As if it somehow gave her the right to pry.

And yet he hadn't done what she'd said. He hadn't walked out. And he wasn't sure why.

"He's not. . . cooperating?"

He stared down at his plate. Set down the fork, his stomach warning against another bite.

"You have no idea," he muttered.

"No, I don't."

He looked up then.

"I have no idea how the magic works, so I wouldn't

begin to offer advice."

"Right now, neither do I." He surprised himself with that, with the fact that he was even having this conversation.

"I'm sorry. I just hope that it's not really the end for Sam."

"Killing him off would be a dramatic ending, except I'm only halfway through."

Damn, he hadn't meant to say that, either. He hadn't even told David he was only halfway through.

"I can't imagine how hard it must be to always come up with something new to happen."

"Right now, impossible."

She finished her last bite of bacon, and he found himself liking the way she savored it. Was that why he was still here, having this conversation he never had with anyone? Just because he liked watching her? When she spoke again, he was surprised he could hear her over the alarm bells going off in his head.

"Maybe you need a list of what won't happen."

He blinked. "What?"

"You know, like Sherlock Holmes. When you've eliminated the impossible. . ." He stared at her. "Sorry, I said no advice, didn't I? I just got that from Mom, she always used what she called 'lists of no' to help her decide about something. A list of things that were off the table, and she said that's where it came from."

"Your mother," he began, slowly, and then his voice died

away because he had no idea what to say about a mother like that.

Or a relationship as close as they obviously had.

"Is the best," she said. "The absolute best. And very, very smart. But even though her advice is good, I shouldn't try to tell you what to do. What do I know about it?"

"You've. . . read them."

"And loved every one of them. But that's a far, far cry from writing one. I don't know how you do it."

He leaned back in his chair. Fiddled with the knife he hadn't really had to use. "Right now, neither do I."

"Then at least a list would be something to do, maybe it'll shake loose something else. Just promise me the first thing on the 'won't happen' list is Sam dying."

He grimaced.

"Or maybe you should write that," she said. "It would show you how awful it would be. Just don't really put it in the book."

He couldn't quite commit to that, either. "I'm afraid if I do that," he said, his voice barely above a whisper, as if speaking the words even quietly would destroy Sam's world, "I won't be able to undo it."

She gave him an odd look, but he couldn't explain. Couldn't explain how actually writing those words, words ending Sam's heartrending young life, would be both torture and release. And that if he did, he was afraid he'd be writing toward that end subconsciously from then on.

"Then try mom's list. It couldn't hurt to try, could it?"

Couldn't hurt to try.

An hour later he was pacing his office. The laptop was on, that damnable cursor blinking on the blank screen that should have been the next chapter. He had notes scattered all over. A corkboard with images tacked up on his left. To his right were the pages of the wiki he'd printed out. He'd belatedly realized he needed one when it became clear there were going to be more than just a couple of books, to make it easier to keep all the details straight in his head. By then he'd discovered some devoted readers had already put one together online, and he'd been saved a lot of work and rereading.

He could see the first page. Sam loved animals, but stayed away from them so he didn't become attached. Was right handed, but had learned to use his left pretty well when his right had been broken before he escaped. He hated sunrises because it meant another day, loved them because it meant he'd survived. And it would get warmer. Loved apples, probably because they were the only thing he could easily steal when he'd been starving.

"You'd have loved that pancake this morning, kid," he muttered to the center photo on the corkboard, of an ordinary looking boy with extraordinary eyes in a too-thin face.

Like I loved that kiss?

And there he was, back at that again. He realized his fingers had stolen up to his mouth, to touch his lips, as if she'd left a trace somehow. He jerked his hand away. He had to stop obsessing about this. About her.

He whirled and grabbed at his chair. Sat down. Opened a new page.

And started to make a list.

Chapter Twenty-Two

KELSEY DRAGGED HER fingers in the water at Booze Kelly's feet as she walked by his statue. It always made her smile. It was one of the things she loved most about this quirky town. Built on whiskey, made famous by boots, scented with lavender, and livened up with some racy lingerie sold out of a former brothel. Nope, not a lot of places with a history like Whiskey River.

She hadn't been into town in a while, so intent had she been on Oliver during the day, and reading in the evening. She'd missed it, so she was taking a walk around the town square just because. And thinking about what she'd just finished doing last night. Reading every one of the Sam Smith books, one after the other. Again.

Because this time she was coming at them in an entirely different way. This time she was reading them knowing Sam's happy ending was in doubt, and this bothered her far more than a fictional character should. Perhaps because she knew for sure now that Sam was indeed an alter-ego of sorts. Maybe she was entangling them too much, but she couldn't help wondering if Sam's predicament was an echo of his creator's. He couldn't see any way out because Declan couldn't.

She paused in front of the bookstore. The display was still there. She stared at the array of books. It hadn't changed, but she had. Because she knew now, not just the stories in the books, but the story behind them.

Some of it, anyway. She had the feeling there was much, much more, and while part of her wanted to learn it all, another part warned her she might not like what she learned.

Be careful what rocks you turn over, Kels, because you never know what you might find underneath.

Her father's advice after she'd nearly been stung by a scorpion had been burned into her mind, although it wasn't until she was older that she understood it in the metaphorical sense as well.

In this case, she wouldn't find any horrors of her own, but the ones that might be hiding would still hurt. She knew that, because she already hurt so much for Declan Kilcoyne—and Declan Bolt, and Crazy Joe—it was a near constant presence.

She grabbed at her cell and hit the speed dial.

"Kelsey! I was just thinking about you," her mother said.

"I love you, Mom."

There was a moment's pause. "Are you all right?"

"I can't call to just say I love you?"

"Of course. And you do, bless you. But you don't usually

lead with it."

"I was just thinking about people who aren't as lucky as I've been, to have you."

Again a pause. "Your new landlord," she said, and it wasn't a question. Her mother didn't miss much. Ever.

"Yes."

"I love you back, Kelsey. You have the biggest heart in the world."

"Second biggest," she corrected, as usual. Her mother laughed, as always.

"I picked up his books."

That surprised her, her mother had little time to read for pleasure. She looked again at the book display in the window, at the cardboard stand up of the skinny kid with the too-old eyes.

"I wanted to see who my girl was dealing with."

"Did you read any?"

Her mother's laugh was rueful this time. "Much more than I planned on. And I was up far too late doing it."

"I know the feeling."

"He's really quite talented. And, as you said, they're not only children's stories. There are layers upon layers."

"Yes."

"And you're right, those stories, of what Sam escaped from. . . they have the ring of brutal truth. I'm not surprised you feel for him."

"Sam? Or Declan?"

"Yes."

"But he doesn't want me—or anyone—to feel for him."

"Doesn't he? Or does he just say that, because isolation is easier for him?"

"I. . . don't know."

"What are you going to do about it?"

Kelsey laughed. "Why are you assuming I'll be doing anything?"

"Because you're who you are. And because of the way you talk about him, and the way your voice sounds when you do."

"He told me he wasn't one of my rescues."

"He did, did he?"

"Yes." Kelsey sighed. "That was when he told me his father left so he wouldn't kill his mother."

"And left him there to cope, alone?"

"Exactly my question. And I think his, ever since."

"What an awful thing to do. Is she still alive? Or his father?"

"No idea. He hasn't said. Maybe he doesn't know."

"Certainly no reason for him to care, if you're right about some version of Sam's story being his."

"So, what do I do?"

"Do you remember Breanna Carter?"

"I was just thinking about her the other day, and what dad said after we found out her sister was dying."

"And do you remember how you kept at her, being nice,

ignoring her meanness?"

Kelsey did remember. Encouraged by both her parents, she kept pecking at the girl until, at last, Breanna let Kelsey in. They'd become friends, and even closer after Kelsey's father had been killed, and they shared that permanent sort of agony. Some years after Bree's family had had to move away for her sister's treatment, she had gotten a phone call from out of the blue, thanking her. Saying Kelsey was the only thing that had gotten her through that awful time. They still got together every couple of years, their own little ritual of remembrance.

"Are you saying I should do the same here?"

"I'm just saying that, in some ways, what he's been through is even worse. You never, ever questioned your father's love for you, nor Breanna her sister's. It sounds like your guy never had any love to question in the first place."

Kelsey sighed. "I know."

"Just be careful. I don't want you ending up in pain trying to ease his. If he's too closed off, too locked up, he needs professional help."

"He had some, of sorts," she said, thinking of Frank Shipley, who had had the wisdom if not the training of a counselor.

And suddenly, a thought occurred to her. Actually, more struck than occurred, because it seemed so blindingly clear.

Frank. Of course!

"Mom, you're brilliant."

"A given," her mother said with a facetious laugh. "But what did I do?"

"You gave me—and Declan—the answer."

She hurried back to her truck, the idea bubbling over in her head. Of course, maybe it was only brilliant to her. What did she know, after all? But the fact that she wasn't a writer, didn't have the first clue about what it took, didn't mean she couldn't have an idea, did it?

She thought about heading straight to the fortress, as she'd taken to calling it in her head. Would he even answer the door, would he let her in? Just because he had before didn't necessarily mean the door was open to her now.

And that kiss? What did that mean?

She decided, perhaps cravenly, that she would go home first, and check on Oliver. When she got there, she was startled to see someone already with the newest arrival.

Declan.

He was sitting on the railing of the corral. The roan horse, who was already looking much better in just ten days, stood there as Declan rubbed that spot under his jaw.

The horse looked in utter bliss.

The man looked. . . actually happy.

For a moment she just watched them, her heart filling with such warmth and happiness it almost ached with it. Odd how that could happen, she thought, how both ends of the emotional scale could produce similar physical reactions.

She glanced over at the fence between his place and hers.

Which was still his, she reminded herself. There was no sign of a vehicle. She realized then that he was wearing running shoes and nylon running pants, and deduced he was back to long distances. Obviously, he was right and that ankle just locked up on him now and then.

She continued to watch man and horse, wondering about wounded souls recognizing each other. For a moment, she pondered just leaving them be, but found it more than she could manage. And felt gratified—and silly about that fact— when he didn't take off the moment he saw her coming.

So that's all it takes? That he doesn't run screaming when he sees you? You are in so much trouble, girl. . .

And yet she kept going.

Chapter Twenty-Three

"HE REALLY LIKES you. He'll be ready to go soon, you should adopt him."

Declan stopped the rhythmic caress. Oliver nudged him for more. When it wasn't immediately forthcoming, the horse took a step toward Kelsey, sniffing intently.

"Fickle," Declan said.

"You stopped," she pointed out, hoping he wasn't going to retreat into that stiffness again. "And I'm the one who's been feeding him most. And you're the only other one he's interested in."

He slid from the rail to the ground. "I told you, I'll never have another horse."

"Why? You obviously love them, they respond to you."

"Not up for discussion."

"How long is that list of things not up for discussion?"

He looked at her for a long, silent moment. "Shorter than it used to be. With you, anyway."

Her heart gave a little skip. He stared at her. The air between them suddenly felt like a thunderstorm was moving in. Charged, electric. . . dangerous.

"Don't think," she said, her voice soft, "that I don't know the size of that compliment."

"I know you do." His voice was nearly as soft as hers had been. And he was looking at her in a way she'd seen once before. Right before he'd kissed her. "Kelsey?"

"Yes."

It was much more than just a response to her name, and he knew it. And then he was kissing her. It wasn't like the first time. That had clearly been an impulse she thought he'd regretted. This was with full intent, even if that intent was to learn if it would be like the first time, hot and fierce.

It wasn't.

It was more.

As if the memory of that first time had already kindled the fire, it erupted instantly. Kelsey heard a tiny sound of shock and pleasure she belatedly realized had come from her. The feel of his mouth on hers was suddenly the most important thing in the world, the taste of him the sweetest, the heat of him the hottest.

She wanted to be closer, wanted to feel all of his heat. Even as she thought it, he pulled her against him, knee to mouth. His hands dove into her hair, pulling strands loose from her braid. He deepened the kiss, probing gently yet insistently with his tongue. She opened for him without a thought of resistance because, in truth, she'd been waiting for this, longing for this since the first time.

She tasted him in turn, heard him groan low in his throat. His hands slipped down her back, to clasp her hips and urge her even closer. She gasped at the feel of already rigid flesh behind his zipper, and felt a flush of turbulent heat ripple through her at the thoughts and images that careened into her mind. She felt almost light-headed with it all, or perhaps it was simply that she'd forgotten how to breathe.

Just as she realized that, he broke the kiss. For a split-second, the only thing she could hear was the hammering of her heart and the sound of deep, rapid breathing it took her a moment to realize was his.

And then a loud, raucous cheer arose, and she realized the men on the work crew had seen them. She wondered if they had any idea who he was. Not who he really was, but who he was known as in town. If they'd have been cheering if they'd realized she'd just been kissed half out of her mind by Crazy Joe, the town recluse.

"Let's get out of here," he muttered.

"Some privacy would be nice," she agreed.

And a split-second later realized that, somewhere in her mind, this decision had already been made. It was probably foolish, maybe as crazy as Whiskey River thought Joe was, but she wanted him. Wanted him in a way she'd never wanted before, and it thrilled her even as it scared her a little.

"You mean that?" She saw in his eyes everything he was asking.

If they left here, now, it would be to one end.

"Somewhat to my surprise, yes."

"You know what you're getting." He said it in the tone of a warning, which she supposed it was.

"Trying to talk me out of it?"

"God, no. But—"

She silenced him with a finger to his lips. "Big girl, Declan. I'll deal." And then, with as much of a smile as she could manage given just touching him, and the thought of touching him in the ways to come, made her shiver, she added, "I'll drive. Faster."

She felt as much as saw and heard him let out a shuddering breath. And then they were in her truck and headed for his fortress.

"Last chance to change your mind," he growled out as she stopped the truck in front of the house.

She laughed. "Oh, way past that."

Her blood was up, singing through her veins. Her mother had always said she would know, as she herself had the first time she'd laid eyes on Eric Blaine. And their life hadn't been a simple thing, no military life was, but two things she had never, ever doubted, that her parents loved her and each other, and that the hard times were worth it.

She was under no illusions. Declan Kilcoyne brought a very different, very deep set of hard times with him, but if she'd learned anything from her mother it was how to endure when things got tough.

Perhaps she could give him some of that, or at least show him some things were worth the risk.

PART OF HIS mind, that part honed by long ago lessons, was screaming alarms about the size of the mistake he was making. He heard them, the warning that no one could be trusted this much, that he was letting her get too close, that this would not be just a casual sharing of bodies.

His body didn't care. If he was honest, neither did the rest of his brain, which said if he couldn't trust Kelsey there was no point in going on anyway, that he didn't want her as close as she already was, he wanted her closer, and that there had been nothing casual about this since the day she'd charged up to storm his fortress when she thought he was Crazy Joe.

Hell, maybe he was Crazy Joe.

He'd never realized how hard it was to move normally when you were aroused to the point of pain. Maybe because he'd never been so stirred up, so hot, so damned hard before. He stopped six feet inside the door. Swore, low and harsh.

"Not making it upstairs."

"Not required." She sounded breathless and, when he looked at her, he saw an answering heat that stoked his own even higher.

The difference. This was the difference, when you cared.

He thought it rather numbly, in that part of his brain that was shutting down as the part demanding he end this ache now took over. He just managed to remember the condom in his wallet, had to hope it wasn't too old to work.

They made it to the couch, barely. They shed clothes crazily, shoes and boots, socks, shirts. And then she was before him wearing only a simple yet somehow gorgeous bra with a tiny bit of lace trim, and cotton panties that should have been plain but had a high-cut leg that put them in different territory altogether. On her, at least. God, those legs. . .

He wanted between them. He wanted them wrapped around him. And he wanted her writhing with pleasure and the need for more, ever more.

Another alarm went off in the last second before that part of his mind shut down completely. He was nothing but need now. He fumbled with the clasp of her bra; it had been a very long time. She didn't care, didn't even seem to notice, in fact, helped him to get it loose. It dropped to the floor and her breasts spilled free, luscious curves that would fill his hands. A moment later the practical yet sexy panties followed. And he stopped breathing altogether.

Declan thought he'd never seen or felt or heard anything so hot as a naked Kelsey Blaine reaching for him, tugging at running pants, the sound as the nylon slid under her hands. And then she touched him, stroked her fingers over his swollen cock, and it was all he could do to hold back.

When she moaned, low in her throat, it was nearly all over just at the sound. And he realized that last, feeble alarm his brain had sent had been the equivalent of the words, "life-changing."

And he didn't care. He didn't want his life changed, but he could no more stop now than he could cut off that part of him she was now cupping, holding.

They went down to the couch together. It was awkward, clumsy even, but he didn't care about that either. He cared about nothing but this woman and this ferocious need. He wanted to kiss every inch of her skin, and tried, but he was already too out of control. When he cupped her breast and lifted the already taut peak to his mouth, the sound she made nearly sent him over the edge. He tasted the nub of flesh, flicked it with his tongue until she cried out, and he felt her body fairly ripple as her hips arched in response.

He reached between them, slid a hand down her belly until he found the answering heat. He stroked once, and the slick readiness he found banished the last reservation. She wanted this, wanted him, her body didn't lie.

Kelsey Blaine didn't lie.

"Hurry," she whispered, arching against him again.

He did. He sheathed himself in her in one long, fierce stroke. Barely realized the guttural groan he heard had issued from his own throat. Barely realized anything except that this was the most incredible sensation he'd ever felt, her body hot and tight around him. He shuddered with the power of it and, even as he wished he could stay like this forever, he had to move. He had no choice, it was too deep, too primal, he had to move.

She rose to each thrust, urging him deeper, faster, with tiny cries that seared him in some deep, hidden place never reached before. It was too much, too much, and he knew he was hanging on by a thread.

"I can't. . . stop." It was all he could get out.

And Kelsey clung to him, whispered low and husky. "Don't you dare stop."

He drove deep again, again, and a third time. In the moment she cried out his name he felt a sudden clenching, making her even tighter around him. This was all new for him, and it took him a second to realize he was feeling, actually feeling her come around him.

Just the thought severed the last thread of his control. He buried himself in her one last time and let go. Felt the rushing, boiling heat of an explosion unlike anything he'd ever experienced. On and on, until he thought he must have poured every last bit of himself into her.

He collapsed atop her, drained. Spent. And yet somehow it felt as if he'd found the place he'd only dreamed of as a scared kid. The place he'd never really had. The place his child's mind only had one word for, although he'd never known it in the way others did.

Home.

Chapter Twenty-Four

THEY'D MADE IT to bed, finally. And each time they'd come together had been as fiery as the first. In between, he'd worked hard at reestablishing his distance, his safety zone, and done his best to quash the silly, melodramatic thoughts that had swamped him.

It was just that it had been so long, he told himself. He'd forgotten how good sex could be when you were attracted to someone. And he wouldn't deny that he was attracted to Kelsey. A lot.

But he was also who he was, and he wouldn't deny that, either. She'd known that going in. He'd made sure of that.

He watched her for a moment before he said lightly, "Regrets?"

"Not yet," she answered, stretching in a way he'd already begun to treasure. "Don't make me have any, okay? I feel too good."

He suspected the only way for him to do that was to not talk at all, and while he was quite willing to follow that plan, he doubted she was.

"That's an interesting expression," she said, her tone teasing.

"Just the expression any guy would wear, standing in the middle of a minefield."

"If a wrong word was all it would take, I wouldn't be here in the first place."

It took him a moment to work out what she meant. That if whatever this was between them was that fragile, she never would have gone to bed with him. He realized on some level he'd known that. Kelsey Blaine was not one for casual sex with any guy who came along. No matter what Declan told himself.

The one-two punch hit him hard. For her at least, this had not been casual sex. And he wasn't, to her, just any guy.

Terror shot through him in a white-hot burst.

No, no, no. He didn't want this. Especially from a woman he would really hate to hurt. He should have listened to those warnings.

But he couldn't have stopped. Not then.

He wished she still thought he was just Crazy ol' Joe, that she didn't have any idea who he really was. And then he wondered why. Because it would be easier to walk away?

"Why are you here?"

The words were out before he could stop them, even though he didn't want her to answer. He couldn't read her expression, tried to tell himself that at least meant she wasn't angry. Maybe.

"Why do you think?" she asked.

He grimaced. Said nothing.

"Oh, let me guess."

There was an undertone in her voice he couldn't quite put a name to. She tapped a finger on her chin in a mocking imitation of someone in deep thought. The entire picture was jarred a bit by the fact that she was still naked in his bed, making it difficult to focus on what she was saying.

"Let's see, I'm here because I feel sorry for your miserable past?" She ticked them off, finger to thumb, like a checklist. "Or, no, it's because you're my landlord? No, no, wait, I have it, it's because now I know you're famous, and I'm a celebrity hound!"

He had, in fact, wondered about all of those things at one time or another. And because of that he couldn't meet her gaze. But looking away from her face just made him all the more aware of the lithe, strong body, all long lines and taut curves, the body she'd shared with him, given to him, with an eagerness that drove him mad and a touch of shyness that had made him want to be more careful with her than he'd ever been in his life.

"I just. . ." His voice trailed off, he couldn't think of a damned thing to say. And he'd learned long ago and the hard way that sometimes the best thing to say was nothing.

"If you're trying to insult me enough so that I'll leave and never come back," she said, still with the note he didn't quite get in her voice, "you're on the wrong track. Now if I thought you really believed any of that. . ."

That was just it. He didn't. And he had no idea why. It wasn't in his nature to trust, anyone, but he trusted her. Whatever her reasons for being here, with him, were, they were not those three he dreaded.

"I don't," he finally said.

"All right, then." She sounded satisfied.

And only now that it was gone did he recognize that the undertone in her voice had been caution, as if she'd been leading him through that minefield he'd mentioned.

As in fact she had, he realized.

"You should have taken off running, you know." His voice was low with the effort to keep it even. Why was he even saying it when, at this moment, her doing just that was what he feared most?

And then she rolled over and snuggled up next to him. "And miss this?" she said with a teasing smile.

"How can you. . . you shouldn't settle for. . ."

He took a breath, difficult as it was with so much of her silken skin pressed against him. And began to realize the difference he'd felt before, the difference between a casual hookup between two people who cared for nothing beyond the moment and. . . this, was so vast he wouldn't be able to process it for a while. Yet he felt compelled to get this out. As if he were indeed belatedly heeding the warnings his mind had tried to give.

"Kelsey, all I can give is so much less than you deserve."

She lifted her head. "You do have a way with words. Maybe you should be a writer."

He let out the breath. "I mean it."

"I know." Then, after a moment, she said, "Percentage."

He blinked. "What?"

"If you take, for example, what percent my ex gave me of his total capability for caring, compared to what you give me of your capacity for caring, I'd say it's about twenty to fifty."

He stared at her. "I'm not sure if I'm suddenly in bed with an engineer or you're just saying I'm stunted, caring-wise. Which, by the way, I already knew."

"My dad was basically a logistician," she said. "He taught me to analyze. And I'm not saying stunted. That implies permanent. I think you just have a big empty place you need to fill."

"And you're just the woman to fill it?" He said the cliché rather bitingly, but she didn't react to his tone.

She merely shook her head. "Only you can do that. But you have to open the gates, as it were."

He looked pointedly at them both, sprawled naked on his bed.

"Oh," she said cheerfully, "this is a good beginning. You've got a long way to go, though."

That, he thought, was no less than the truth. He'd always accepted that. But the thought that he could undo some of the damage done was a new one; he'd always been focused on how to live with it, how not to get hurt more, not how to change himself. He would have said it couldn't be done.

Had said it.

But that was before he'd met Kelsey Blaine.

And, suddenly, the need welled up in him again. And this time, seeming almost resigned, the warning part of his brain told him to get while the getting was good. That it wouldn't last, because nothing good ever did.

That it had been his charming mother who had preached that seemed sourly fitting just now.

He moved then, quickly, rolling her on top of him. Her breasts were pressed against his chest, and he promised himself he was going to spend a long time with them in a moment.

"Then I'd better get started," he said roughly.

"Yes," she said simply.

And stretched sinuously, in essence caressing him with her entire body. And then she kissed him, the first time she had begun it. And that thrilled him way beyond reason.

That was his last coherent thought.

He woke up much later, a little stunned that he'd dozed off in the middle of the day. But then, he had been pretty busy all morning. He managed not to grin, although barely.

He sat up. He felt oddly light, as if he hadn't eaten all day. Thought about food, but that would necessitate leaving the bed, and that didn't appeal at all. By the time he figured out this new lightness had nothing to do with real food and everything to do with the tempting morsel beside him, she was sitting up beside him.

He saw her glance at the pen and pad he kept on the nightstand.

"Late night ideas?" she guessed.

"Not lately," he said with a grimace.

It was the bleak truth; he hadn't had a decent idea here or anywhere else for weeks. Well, except for getting her here. That was way beyond decent. He was just still surprised she'd agreed.

"You write in the tower, don't you?"

"Not lately," he repeated. He'd eliminated possibilities, with her list idea, but still had no solution.

She gave him an exaggeratedly sad look. "Still stuck?"

He didn't want to talk about this. Not even to her.

"Declan Kilcoyne," she said, the combination of her saying his full name and her sharp tone making him draw back slightly. "If this is where you think you can give me the 'just because we had sex doesn't mean you get to pry,' speech, think again."

He blinked. Because his mind had indeed wandered in that direction. "Gotten that speech before, have you?"

"No. I don't put myself in that position. My mother warned me a long time ago about guys like that."

"And what makes you think I'm not one of them?"

She shrugged. "I think you're just uncomfortable with this. It's new."

"You really think you have me figured out, don't you?"

"So I'm wrong?"

"Why are you so sure you're right?"

"Because you keep answering questions with questions."

Well, she had him there.

"I still think you should adopt Oliver."

He drew back at the sudden change of subject. It was a change of subject, wasn't it?

"I told you, never again."

"Why? Strictly a. . . business question. It is my job, after all."

He let out a long breath. "Your job to talk people who don't want a horse into adopting one? Isn't that counterproductive?"

"You'd never neglect him the way they did," she said. "But my question was why don't you want one? I'd think long, solitary rides with lots of time to think would be appealing."

He was startled by the sudden stab of longing that went through him. It was appealing. And, again, she had jolted him out of old thought patterns and into contemplating new ones. If only that could translate to new ideas elsewhere. . .

He made an impulsive decision. Another rarity. "Come on," he said, rolling out of bed and pulling on the jeans he'd tossed over a chair. She didn't question, just tugged on her own clothes and, were he not so sated, he would have regretted that.

But probably not nearly as much as he was going to regret this.

Chapter Twenty-Five

H E TOOK HER up the curving stairway, for the full effect. And when he glanced at her, she was smiling, whether at the novelty of the tower or the fact that he was taking her to the inner sanctum, as it were, he didn't know. Decided he didn't care; the smile was enough.

When they reached the office, she stopped dead one step inside. Her head turned as she scanned the circular room. He saw her gaze snag on the windows, the scope, his story boards, and the poster of his first book cover on the far wall.

"Oh, it's perfect!"

"It's neater than it usually is." He couldn't help his rather sour tone in contrast to her delight. "Since I can't write, I've had lots of time to tidy up."

She began to walk around the perimeter of the room. He realized the scope was pointed toward her place, and hoped she wouldn't notice. He hadn't been spying on her—in fact, the last time he'd used it he'd been watching Oliver, fascinated by the animal's tentative steps into a better life—but he suddenly felt like a stalker.

She stopped in front of the poster of the book cover. It was dramatic, eye-catching, and he knew the artwork was a large part of that first book's success.

"Why Bolt?" she asked, looking at the name.

He didn't want to go there. Tried to dodge. "Why not?"

"Answering a question with a question again?"

He sighed. She was relentless. Or it seemed that way. Maybe because no one had pushed him like this in a very long time. No one since Frank.

No one had cared enough to push.

Kelsey cared. A lot. She would never have gone to bed with him otherwise.

Just because we had sex doesn't mean you get to pry.

The words she'd warned him not to say hovered. He bit them back. Not because of her warning but because she deserved better. And with the strangest sense of stepping off a cliff, he answered her.

"He was my horse. As a kid."

She smiled, clearly liking that he'd taken the name for that reason. "So you did have one."

"For a while."

"What happened?"

He took in another deep breath to steady himself. "My mother shot him."

Her eyes widened. He saw the shock in them, and more, he saw the anger. Somehow that made it all right, that he'd brought her here, that he'd told her.

"She said he was useless and not worth saving. Just like me."

Kelsey expression changed from anger to something deeper, fiercer, when he added those last words. And when she spoke there was a note of venom in her voice he never would have thought her capable of.

"I have never," she said, fairly spitting the words out, "wanted to kill another human being but, for her, I think I would make an exception."

Her reaction told him many things, things he would have to analyze later, but right now all he knew was he felt a sort of relief. That lightness again, that seemed inextricably linked to her.

"Too late," he said.

"She's dead?"

He nodded. "Couple of years ago."

"Good." She said it with a fierceness that surprised him. And warmed him. Then, looking at the poster on the wall, asked, "Did she know?"

"No."

She turned back to him. "Why not? Didn't you want her to see how wrong she was, what a success you were?"

"Not enough to give her another shot at me. So I hid behind a pen name and the trust. Because I knew she would have. . . destroyed it somehow. Or me."

She looked thoughtful. Then nodded. "She probably would have perverted it all anyway. Suddenly started bragging about her rich, successful son."

And, yet again, she voiced his exact thoughts. His mother would have loved that, and would have claimed as much of the credit for it as she could. "Not to mention coming at me for money."

He ran his thumb along the edge of the stack of printer paper on the desk, bending the corners and letting them snap back into place.

"I used to wonder why she didn't just abort me," he said, before he realized the words were forming. "Then I realized the fact that she hadn't must mean she'd wanted a child. Just. . ."

He heard Kelsey's breath catch as his words died away. "Not you," she finished in a whisper.

"Obviously I didn't live up to her expectations." His mouth twisted. "Ever."

She studied him for a moment. "But you did eventually run away. That's why the first Sam story is so real, because you did it first."

"Sam's braver, tougher, smarter than I am. He actually does what I only wished I could do. I stayed until I was thirteen because I was a coward."

She laughed. It wasn't a nasty laugh, or mocking, but somehow heartening. "I swear, only you could call escaping an ogre like that at thirteen cowardly."

He didn't know what to say, how to thank her for the way she was making him feel. So he said nothing.

"What about Frank?" she asked after a moment.

He was unable to look at her, but also unable to stop. It was as if she'd turned the spigot and it had broken, leaving no way to stop the flow of the story he'd never completely told to anyone.

"He was why I ran. He finally pulled me out of there, called in protective services. The court ordered her to be allowed visits. That's when she told me she was going to kill him if he kept interfering. I knew she meant it, and I couldn't risk that, not when he'd done so much already."

"Did you tell him?"

"I wrote him a note, gave it to another cop to give to him. Then I faked being sick at school, they took me to the nurse, and I ran."

"He must have been worried about you."

"I sort of kept in touch. I didn't want to risk snail mail and a postmark so when I could I sent him an email."

"Did he answer?"

He nodded. "He said he understood, but he was afraid for me. Said he'd come and get me, wherever I was, if I'd let him. I couldn't."

"Because of her."

"I think even with all he knew, he underestimated her. What she was capable of. But I didn't."

"He was a cop," she said gently.

He grimaced. "Yeah. And I was thirteen. I wasn't thinking in terms of he could take care of himself."

"She must have seemed. . . undefeatable to you then. Monolithic."

And again she put the exact words to what he'd felt back then. And again his words failed him, he who had used them so well for years now. He just looked at her, shaking his head in wonder at her.

"Ah, Kels. . ."

She shot him a sideways look at the shortening of her name. "Yes, Deck?"

He blinked, startled. "That's what Frank used to call me."

"And my father called me Kels."

"So. . . I shouldn't?"

"Should I?"

"I. . . it's fine. For you."

"Ditto. For you."

He felt an odd sensation, the increasing lightness again, as if the exchange that was on the surface nothing more than a small step was in fact something more. Much more.

She walked over to his desk, ran a finger over his closed laptop. Then she turned to look at him. "I read the books again."

He drew his head back slightly, startled at the abrupt shift. "Again? All four of them?"

She nodded. Gave him a crooked smile that kindled the warmth down deep that had yet to fully ebb since she'd come home with him. "That's the process, isn't it? From what I've seen online, kids read them repeatedly."

He let out a low, short laugh. "Yeah. They write me, about the strangest little details."

"Do you answer?"

"All I can." His mouth quirked. "Found my lawyer through one of the first fan letters I got. The kid was so straight arrow and honest I figured his dad must be the same." He shook his head. "They ask about stuff that doesn't really matter, or that I even forgot putting in there. Sometimes I have to go back and read myself to remember it."

She smiled again, wider this time. "Because to them, Sam is alive."

"I guess."

"That's why you can't kill him, you know," she said, her tone casual. "Somewhere there are kids in circumstances like yours, and Sam may be the only thing that keeps them hanging on. And the only lessons, the only warnings they'll heed." She turned, leaned back against the edge of his desk. "But then, you know that. It's why you wrote them, isn't it?"

He knew he was staring at her. He couldn't help it. How did she do this, how did she know all this? How could she know that was why he'd had the idea to write the books in the first place, because there were kids out there in the same kind of hell? And that he kept writing them as much as warning as anything, hoping they would learn as Sam had, that people you trust can betray you, people who pretend to be nice sometimes aren't, and in the end you're responsible for you.

She was, as Frank had often said, rattling his cage. In a big way.

Of course, Frank had also said Declan held the key to that cage; all he had to do was be brave enough to use it.

"How," he said carefully, "could you know that?"

"I told you, I read them again. This time knowing you a little better." He saw her take in a deep breath. "And I think I know what's wrong. Why Sam—and you—are stuck."

He stiffened slightly. She stopped. He waited. She held his gaze, silently.

"Well?"

He sounded defensive even to himself. And he wasn't sure why, it wasn't like she was some stranger telling him how or what to write, or trespassing on his creative muse or some other pretentious conceit. Hell, his muse was off on a binge somewhere, and had been for weeks.

"If you're going to be angry," she said, "I'll just keep my ideas to myself. I'm not the writer, you are."

"Not lately," he said, wondering when that had become his catchphrase. "Tell me."

She studied him for a moment, and he realized he was standing with his arms crossed over his chest, as if he were protecting himself from whatever she was going to say. He had never allowed anyone else into his writing process, other than his editor. Sam was his, spoke with his voice, succeed or fail.

He uncrossed them. He had asked, after all. And Kelsey was smart, clever, and had more instinctive understanding than anyone he'd ever known. If he was ever going to ask advice from anyone, it would be her. And he surely needed. . . something.

"There's something missing. Something that's been steadily dwindling through the series," she said. "It was there at the beginning, at least a bit of it. But now. . ."

She paused. Looked at him as if she weren't sure she should go on. If it was anything else, he'd play the game, coax her. But this was his work, and it was, silly as it sounded, sacred.

So he said only, rather bluntly, "What?"

She gave him a sad smile. "Hope."

He nearly snorted aloud. "That again. Like hope ever changed anything."

"No. It doesn't. Hasn't. Hope can't change anything. It's utterly useless. Except for one thing."

"Which is?"

"Sometimes it's the only thing that keeps us going."

"It's a lie."

"A lot of the time, yes. But think about those kids. Reading Sam's story, seeing him get battered time after time, seeing the hope drain out of him. They're getting it, understanding, it's why they're so anxious for the next book because surely this will be the one where he's saved, where their own hope comes true. . ."

"They'll learn."

"Yes, they will. Life will teach them," she said, and he suddenly remembered just how much she knew about losing hope.

"Kels," he began, then stopped to savor the tiny smile that curved her mouth when he used the name.

"Do you really want to be the one to teach them that hope is mostly useless?"

"I don't write fairy tales. And I'm not starting now."

"No, you don't. And that's not what I'm saying."

He started to pace, only half-aware he was tracking the same path he had for weeks now, to the window without looking out, then back to the wall where that framed book poster taunted him.

"Sam's in a hole so deep there's no way out. He's in bigger trouble than I know how to get him out of. And he's tired of playing the game. He's looking at deep water and thinking if he swam until he was exhausted and too far from shore to get back, then the decision would be made for him."

He wondered if she would find it odd, that he spoke of Sam as if he were real. Glanced at her. She didn't look surprised, or even amused. Just intent. And intense.

"Exactly," she said. "And don't think your readers, those kids, don't sense that. And if you kill off that boy they all love, some of them will give up hope as well."

He whirled back to face her. "Do you think I don't know that? I read their letters, I know some of them are in a hell like I was, I know some of them are walking a knife edge, and one push could send them over."

"Then don't betray them. Or the other kids who are trying to help them, because they've read Sam's story and know what to look for now."

She made it sound so simple. What the hell, she wasn't the one sitting there at that laptop, day after day, staring at a blank page and—the irony bit deep—hoping for words that weren't there. Anger spiked through him.

"Don't you get it? It's just not there."

"Sam doesn't trust anyone. Just like you."

And maybe until he does, you can't. "There is no one to trust. I can't save him."

"But someone can."

"No one can."

"Someone saved you."

He frowned. "What are you saying?"

"Simple," she said, holding his gaze steadily. "Give him Frank."

Chapter Twenty-Six

"*WORDS?*" KELSEY TEXTED. It was five minutes before she got an answer. She spent it dressing after her shower, and was done except for her boots when the incoming text alert chirped.

"*Yes.*"

"*Food?*" she sent back.

Another pause. A long one. Finally she sent another.

"*You can't remember when you ate last, right?*"

An emoticon came back at her, with its tongue hanging out and its eyes crossed. He'd been holed up for three days now. She'd walked cautiously, not wanting to disturb the flow, if that was what it was, but she missed him. She didn't know much about the care and feeding of a writer, but there were people out there who did, and she didn't hesitate to ask for advice. She'd haunted online groups until she had a good idea of what to do, and more importantly what not to. So rather than going over and pounding on his door, yesterday, she'd found his number in her call log and texted him to ask if he was okay. He'd sent back, "*Working.*" And then a moment later, *"Thanks to you."*

She felt as if she'd been given some sort of precious award. She'd sent back an acknowledgment and left him alone.

As she would now. For the most part.

"Go back to work," she sent.

He didn't answer that one. She didn't care. It was enough that she'd helped, that her idea had broken the logjam.

She headed out to check on the horses. They'd finished the hay she'd put out this morning. The water trough was still full, and gleamed thanks to her messy job of scouring it out this morning. It wasn't a fun job, but they had clean water and she wouldn't need to do it again for a while. She was glad she'd done it before taking a shower though, because she'd worked up quite a sweat.

She went back to the trailer and built a rather monstrous sandwich out of whatever looked good, including a layer of leftover steak she sliced into strips. She wrapped it in foil and put it in small grocery bag, along with some chips and an apple. She thought for a moment, then added the cookie she'd bought on a whim yesterday, a big affair the shape of Texas and frosted in red, white and blue with the Lone Star neatly added in the blue stripe.

That should do it, she thought as she folded the bag closed. And it would keep her from eating that silly cookie; luscious as it looked, she didn't need the calories, while he could certainly use them.

A few minutes later she was standing at his door, realizing she hadn't quite thought about the fact that he was going to have to come downstairs to answer. Which sort of defeated the purpose of not disturbing his work. She thought for a moment, then started to walk around the house to where she could leave the bag on a patio table for him.

The lap pool glistened in the spring sunshine. The reflection danced across the glass of the windows, reminding her rather potently of the day she'd first seen him here. Her mind wanted to dwell on the horror of the scars of abuse, but with an effort she made herself focus on what he'd done, what he'd accomplished despite such an appalling start in life.

She saw some tiny spots of water on the stone decking. As if some time ago someone had gotten out of the pool and walked toward the house, dripping. Then something else registered, that there was the slightest break in the reflection of the water on the windows. She walked over and saw that the sliding patio door wasn't quite shut.

"Well that solves my problem," she said to herself as she slipped inside. Not to mention she felt better about interrupting him if he'd taken enough of a break for a swim.

She made her way up the curved stairs. The office door was closed. She couldn't hear anything through the heavy door. But clearly he was all right, if he'd gone swimming. So she set the bag on the floor, out of the way but where he'd see it, and took out her phone again.

"Food at the door," she sent, and turned to go. She was halfway down the stairs when she heard a sound, then steps, then his voice.

"Kels?"

She turned back. He was standing a few steps behind her, her bag in his hand. Which she barely noticed, since he was wearing low slung jeans only half zipped. And nothing else.

"I brought you lunch," she said, rather unnecessarily.

She tried not to stare, but she hadn't seen him in three days and she was hungry for the sight of him. That he was only half dressed, baring his chest, ribbed abdomen, and the masculine line of his narrow hips, was a bonus. She fought down the heat that blossomed in her at the sight, silently chanting her vow to leave him alone when he was so obviously working again at last.

"I have food," he said.

"Yes. But you'd have to go get it, fix it. Now you don't."

He glanced at the bag, but only for a moment before his brow furrowed.

"I didn't hear you. How'd you get in?"

"Slider. It wasn't latched."

His expression cleared. "Oh. I hit the pool this morning. I was getting stiff, sitting at the desk so much."

"But that's good, right?"

He smiled then, and it was a warm, slow thing, like the

sun rising over the hill country. "Yes." He let out a breath. "I've got it all mapped out in my head now. It's going to be okay."

"And Sam's not going to die."

She said it firmly. His smiled widened even more.

"No. Sam's not going to die."

She smiled back then. "Millions will be relieved."

"As long as you are. You gave me the key."

"I just helped you see. And speaking of keys, next time you hit the pool, remember to close the door when you're done."

"I was in a hurry," he said, looking a bit disconcerted for such simple words.

"To get back to work?"

"And to get inside. I'm not an exhibitionist by nature, I just didn't want to take the time to change."

It took her a moment. "You mean I missed a chance to watch you get out of that pool stark naked?"

She widened her eyes and pressed a hand over her heart in a dramatic gesture that was only half in fun. Her pulse really had kicked up at the thought. And, that quickly, his expression changed.

"If you want to see me naked, all you have to do is ask."

Something low and husky had come into his voice and it reminded her so much of how he sounded when he was inside her, driving her mad, that she could barely suppress a shiver of reaction. She tried to remember the vow she'd made coming over here.

"I didn't want to disturb you."

"Too late."

"I—"

"Nobody in my life has ever looked at me the way you just did," he said softly.

"You need to get out more," she said, rather weakly.

He shook his head. "I need to stay in. With you."

It took her a moment to steady herself. "Deck?"

"Mmm."

"I'm asking."

For a split-second, his brow furrowed, then cleared. With a slow smile that sent her pulse into overdrive again, he reached down and unzipped his jeans the rest of the way. He had to shift slightly, since he was clearly already fully aroused. Then one push sent them down past his hips, and he kicked his feet clear. For a moment all she could do was stare, and contemplate how all the parts of him came together in that lean, taut, very male way that made it hard to breathe. All of it, all of him, even the scars—perhaps especially the scars—made him the man who moved her as no man ever had.

"I," she said, her voice tight, "have never looked at anyone like this in my life. You make my knees weak."

"Can't have that," he said, coming down the last few steps between them. He handed her the lunch bag. Before she could say a word he'd picked her up in his arms. She looked up at him, then at the bag, rather bemused.

"I'm going to need that later," he promised.

They made it to his bed, but not before an interlude on the stairs taught her how loudly stone walls could echo human voices, especially when she couldn't help crying out his name. Once they were in his rather ascetic bedroom, she set about wringing the same kind of sound from him, ignoring his groaned pleadings to end it, and finally hearing him shout her name in turn in the way that sent her over the edge herself.

And later, for the first time in her life, she discovered the appeal of skinny dipping. It felt more reasonable here, in this place of solitude. And it felt wonderful, she had to admit. Not nearly as wonderful as when he pinned her against the side of the pool and she wrapped her legs around him, but still wonderful.

"I begin to see the advantage," she said lazily when they were spent yet again, "of never having people dropping in unexpectedly."

"You did."

"If you didn't expect me, then you've got a bit more to learn."

"I've got a lot more to learn," he said, nuzzling her neck while his hands slipped up to cup her breasts.

"Insatiable?" she suggested with a teasing laugh.

"Ravenous," he answered in a low growl that sent fire licking along her nerves.

It amazed her how it could possibly still happen so fast, so fierce, even after the hours they'd spent already, learning everything there was to learn about each other's responses.

And when his body arrowed into hers that last time, she thought she wouldn't care if she drowned here right now, because surely nothing could ever top this.

After a few minutes to steady his breathing, he pulled himself out of the pool with a smooth, easy motion that spoke of what she already knew; he might be lean, almost wiry, with the body of the runner he was, but he also had some impressive upper body strength. Which he would, she knew, momentarily use to help her out of the pool.

In the moment before he turned, his left ankle was directly in front of her eyes. She saw the shiny band of the old scar, from whatever injury caused it to occasionally lock up on him as it had that day at the river.

She had seen it before, but hadn't really studied it. After all, most times when it was visible to her she was otherwise occupied, exploring the wonder they'd discovered, the unexpected joy two in tune bodies could give. But now she couldn't help but study it, couldn't help but notice how. . . even it was. Not some jagged tear or surgical scar, but an even band of shiny, damaged skin that wrapped around the entire joint.

"Pretty, isn't it?" he said as he pulled her up onto the pool deck beside him.

Should she be embarrassed for having stared so blatantly

that he'd noticed? Weren't they past that? If he still wouldn't share that kind of thing, then she was in way over her head. So she asked.

"What happened?"

He let go of her hand. Took a step back. "Nothing."

So apparently they weren't past it. *What are you doing here, spending every spare moment thinking about him, having sex with him time after time, practically falling in love with him, when he won't share this? Didn't he realize pain shared was pain lightened?*

"Deck—"

His jaw tightened. "It's what happens when you're shackled to the floor, and then you outgrow them. And this"—he held out his left arm, the one that didn't quite hang right—"is what happens when someone breaks it and it's never set."

She stared at him. There was nothing but truth in his expression, in his eyes. It had been true. Sam's torture had been his. She felt a wrenching, horrifying anguish that was unlike anything she'd ever felt before. She was in agony for him, but even so knew it was nothing compared to the agony he himself had gone through. And at the hands of the one person he should have been able to trust.

She couldn't bear it. She whirled and darted into the house, into the powder room just inside the patio door. She closed the door behind her and sank down on the cool tile floor, tears already streaming down her face. She didn't even try to stop them, she knew she couldn't.

Her eyes were burning painfully by the time the door opened. In her distress she hadn't locked it. He was standing there, looking down at her impassively. He leaned in and set a pile of neatly folded clothing on the floor beside her. Hers. Clothing that had been strewn all over the hallway and his bedroom, the last time she'd seen them.

He dropped her boots beside them. His expression was almost cold now.

"What are you telling me?" she asked.

"I know how ugly it is. And it's nothing compared to the inside. So get out while you can."

"Wait. . . you think. . . what do you think? That I was repelled by that scar?"

"Who wouldn't be? I am."

She got to her feet, slowly.

"Joseph Declan Kilcoyne, you are such an ass."

His brows lowered. "Never denied that."

"You can't really think this had anything to do that."

He blinked then. "You couldn't get away fast enough."

"Because I knew I was going to cry! And I was afraid you'd think it was pity again when, in fact, it's pain and shock and empathy, and so much anger it made me want to throw up."

He looked so stunned she felt a rush of all those emotions all over again.

"Kelsey," he said, his voice trailing away.

"Don't you get it?" she demanded. "It's not pity, it's never been pity. You're many things, but pitiful is not even on the list."

"You're really mad." His tone was full of wonder.

"Damned right I am. If she wasn't already dead—"

He moved suddenly, pulling her into his arms. He didn't kiss her, or caress her, just held her. Tightly, as if he were afraid she would somehow slip out of his grasp. And in that moment the embrace became so much more than even their intense sex had been, as if it were some kind of significant turning point.

For a long time they just stood there. She said nothing, and neither did he. Words would have been superfluous at that moment.

By the time they got to the sandwich she'd brought he insisted on sharing with her. She accepted because her stomach was growling, since it was now late afternoon. They laughed at their own appetites, memories of how they'd built them alive between them, the new closeness lasting.

She enjoyed watching him dig around in the big stainless steel fridge that was an odd sort of contrast to the rough stone walls of the kitchen, which in turn were a contrast to the smooth, veined granite counters, which all seemed to contrast with the heavily grained hickory cabinets.

When he withdrew from the fridge with two bottles, he noticed her looking around.

"A bit much, isn't it," he said, and it wasn't a question.

"Lots of textures and patterns in one room," she said

neutrally.

His mouth quirked. "I don't spend much time in here."

Kelsey didn't answer, she was staring at the bottle he'd set in front of her. "Cream soda?"

He frowned. "You said you liked it."

"I do." And she had said it. She just hadn't expected him to not only remember it, but stock it. "You didn't buy this just for me, did you?"

"I only added it to the list. True's sister handles the shopping."

She accepted that as a yes, given he'd only denied physically shopping. She felt inordinately flattered, for such a small thing.

"Who puts gas in your car?"

"I do." His mouth quirked. "There's a holding tank underground behind the barn."

She was nearly laughing now. "And who fills that?"

"True usually handles that."

"You must leave here sometimes," she said. "Don't you have meetings, like with your agent or editor or something?"

"Video conference."

"Wow. You have this eccentric artist thing down, don't you?"

He toyed with condensation on the side of his own bottle of soda. "I'm not eccentric, Kels."

"Unsociable, then."

"Not unsociable. I'm antisocial."

She studied him for a moment. "What's the difference?"

"Not liking it, and actively avoiding it."

"You are the wordsmith."

"Words mean things."

The things he had told her swirled around in her mind. "Yes," she said softly, "they do. Words like useless, and not worth saving."

He went very still. She sensed her next words were very important, and her voice went down to almost a whisper.

"I don't think I have ever seen a heartless, evil person so thoroughly proven wrong. And when I think of what you had to overcome to be the worldwide success you are, how generous you are with what you've earned. . . you are a remarkable man, Declan Kilcoyne. Or Bolt. In either hat."

He didn't look at her. His hand wrapped around the bottle until his knuckles were white. It stabbed at her that he was so uncomfortable with the praise, that even now some part of him didn't believe, didn't think himself worthy.

"And I'd like you to put on whichever hat you want, and come with me to the town barbecue."

He was shaking his head before she even finished. "No."

"Why not?"

"You know why. I don't. . . do that."

"Correction. You're in the habit of not doing that."

"It's not just a habit."

"Then what? A protective mechanism?"

He shrugged.

She was risking him shutting down, shutting her out again but, in the middle of her assessment of him, she'd come to another realization. And foolish as it was, she didn't want to hide it.

"You're a complicated man, Deck. With reason. And brilliant. And more generous than anyone ever was to you, except Frank. And incredibly sexy, in that deep sort of way that never wears off."

His gaze flicked to her face, as if in disbelief, but she also saw a trace of something else there. As if he were pleased at her words, but still didn't believe them. She kept going, as much for his sake as for hers; he needed to hear this as much as she needed to say it.

"When I first realized the truth, I admired you for it. And that feeling grew the more I learned about you. But now it's more than admiration. A lot more."

He finally spoke. His voice was low, rough. "Don't worry. You'll get over it."

"No. I won't."

"You forgot to mention the other thing about me. That I'm not just antisocial I'm a pain in the ass. Or just an ass, as you said."

"You have your moments. I've learned to deal."

He finally met her gaze, held it. "What do you want from me?"

And there it was. She hesitated, wishing more than anything she hadn't started this, seriously contemplating just saying, "Never mind," and going on as before. But the realization she'd just had, and her own innate honesty, wouldn't let her.

"Not so very much more than you've already given."

"You figure I owe you? Because you helped?" he asked, gesturing in the direction of the tower and his office.

"No. Although I'm glad I helped, that was selfish. I wanted more Sam."

She knew for sure she'd seen gratification in his expression then.

His words confirmed that. "Thank you."

She steadied herself and went on. "I care for you, Deck. A lot. I could easily fall in love with you. So if this is just some. . . some way to scratch an itch without having to leave your sanctuary, I want to know now."

Something flashed in his eyes, something different, fierce. She wished she could believe it was because he felt the same way she did.

But he said only, "Is that really what you think?"

"What should I think? You seem determined to keep us a secret, to never be seen in public with me."

His jaw tightened. "Did you ever stop to think that might be for your sake? You saw how the work crew reacted to just me kissing you. You want the whole town to know you're with Crazy Joe?"

By now she'd gotten used to the fact that he was Declan Kilcoyne, aka Bolt, and she'd almost forgotten that no one else in Whiskey River knew that. But then, no one in Whiskey River knew he wasn't really crazy, either.

"I might believe that, except for the fact that that excuse just lets you continue as you always have. You just don't want to have to actually put a foot out into the real world."

"I've been there. It's overrated."

"Parts of it, yes. But the good parts are so good, they deserve a chance. And maybe," she added, "I want it to be seen that you're not really crazy."

He let out a compressed breath. "You sure about that?"

She reached out, touched his cheek. He closed his eyes. "Are you asking where the line is between reclusive and crazy?"

"I'm not sure there is one for me anymore."

"There is a line, but it's between being of the world or not. And right now I'm on one side, and you're on the other."

His eyes snapped open. "So. . . you're leaving, is that it?"

The dullness she saw growing in his eyes then made her heart ache. An hour ago he'd tried to throw her out, and she realized that had been self-protection, that he'd wanted to be able to tell himself he'd done it, not her.

"That's what you expect, isn't it? To be abandoned? Again?"

"You do what you have to do."

She wasn't sure if that was instruction to her or merely a philosophical observation. With this man either—or both—

seemed possible.

"I'm going nowhere but home, Declan." She gestured in the direction of her place. "And that's where I'll be if and when you decide I'm worth the risk."

Chapter Twenty-Seven

H E AWOKE TO the roll of thunder.

He listened for a moment, eyes still closed, but heard no sound of rain. Just a low hum that sounded like static. He realized he was slumped rather uncomfortably in the chair. He'd given up on actual sleep—in his bed anyway, without Kelsey—at about three AM. He shied away from the great room that held the couch where they'd first made love, and retreated to the media room to watch something mindless on the bigger flat screen. An overwrought reality show did what nothing else had been able to and put him to sleep.

He resisted opening his eyes. He didn't want to be awake. He didn't want to know what time it was. Didn't want to get up and walk into the room where he'd last seen her, before she'd turned and walked out. From him, and all his craziness.

I'm going nowhere but home, Declan. And that's where I'll be if and when you decide I'm worth the risk.

The risk. Of venturing back into the world? Into life outside his fortress? Into a life full of other people? Because he knew that was what she was asking for. He even understood. She had a normal life, and his was not. He couldn't ask her to narrow hers down to fit into his. But he couldn't take the step she wanted. It had been too long and he'd isolated himself too much. He was safe here, like this.

Sam's braver, tougher, smarter than I am. He actually does what I only wished I could do.

His own words echoed in his head. Did he wish he could do this? Really?

Light flashed, bright enough to be seen even through closed eyes. He opened them. A snowy TV screen flickered. He shut it off. Sat in the unlit room as the thunder rolled again. He did his best thinking that way, with exterior distractions lost in the darkness.

As ultimatums went, this was an iron fist in the proverbial velvet glove. She hadn't ordered him to choose. She hadn't said it was the breaking point. She had merely asked him to decide if she, they, were worth the risk.

Not so long ago he would have sworn, instantly, that nothing was worth it. And it would have been true. Only his work had such value to him, and he didn't need to be in the world to do it, only of the world. And participating at a distance had served him just fine for a long time.

But Kelsey had somehow breached that barrier. She—

Another flash. And after a moment the thunder. Closer. He got up then, steeled himself, and went into the great room and over to the windows. Still no rain. Not making it to the ground anyway.

He wondered which way the storm was coming from. Which way it was going. After a moment of watching from here, he headed up the tower, figuring the stone was safe enough. He stepped into his office and walked to the narrow windows. Oddly, the sky to the east was clear enough that he could see the water of the river gleaming. To the north, the starry sky gave way to a blank, towering blackness that he guessed had to be the edge of the storm.

He walked to his desk, unplugged his laptop, just to be safe. He and Sam were rolling now, the path clear, and he didn't want to lose that. As an extra, no doubt unnecessary, precaution he pocketed the USB drive he backed up to. He didn't want that fried, either. Another copy was stored safely online, but he'd learned the hard way about redundancy.

Another flash. Another rumble. He hadn't wanted to, but he went to the other window. And there it was, visible even at night, hulking, hovering, its thick darkness alive with threads of flashing energy. Was Kelsey awake? She must be, no one could sleep through this, and it was practically over her head. Did thunderstorms, even dry ones, bother her? Was she afraid?

He felt the urge to go to her, wishing now he'd never let her go, even if she didn't want to be here, didn't want to be with him. She'd be safe here. From the storm, anyway. He turned away from the window. He couldn't bear to even look that direction, because it only made the scene before she'd gone play over and over in his head, as it did every time he thought of it. She had every right, she—

A brilliant flash cut off his tangled thoughts. On its heels thunder cracked, so loud and close it rattled the windows. He could have sworn he felt a thump, and the tingle of electricity running over his skin. That one had practically been on top of him.

He held his breath, frozen, waiting, half-expecting the tower to crumble around him.

Just what you deserve.

The words, heard in a voice he'd thought buried forever, lashed at him.

"No," he shouted into the momentarily silent office. "You do not get to be here. Not here."

Useless. Worthless. Just like this damned horse.

The echo of the shot in his mind was as loud as the thunder outside.

"You're wrong," he whispered now, less certain.

I don't think I have ever seen a heartless, evil person so thoroughly proven wrong.

Kelsey's words did what nothing else had been able to. They sent the haunting voice back into the fetid, ugly cell where it belonged. And locked the door so thoroughly he thought, for the first time in his life, that he just might not ever hear it again.

He stood there, nearly gasping as he broke free of the hissing voice, feeling suddenly as electric as the storm outside. As if the storm had shocked to life some dormant part of him that had never had free rein before.

"You don't get this, either," he said aloud. "You don't get to ruin the best thing that's ever happened to me."

He spun around, headed for the west window. Going out there right now would be insane, but he wanted to get to Kelsey more than anything right now. Not just to be sure she was all right in the storm, but to tell her he'd known all along she was worth the risk, he just needed to get some crap out of the way first. The moment it passed he would go. In fact, he'd start counting the time between flash and noise, and when it got to—

His rushed thoughts slammed to a halt as he reached the window. A new kind of light danced in the darkness. Close, too close, to Kelsey.

Fire.

Chapter Twenty-Eight

OLIVER, KELSEY THOUGHT, was a Godsend. The horse was remarkably calm despite the storm, and his stoic attitude was the only thing keeping the others from panicking.

Including her after that last strike. It had been much, much too close.

Wearily, she pulled her boots back on. She'd never bothered to undress, figuring it was going to be a long, noisy night and she needed to be ready to go at a second's notice. In a way she was glad of the storm; it helped keep her mind off what she'd done. She'd gambled and lost, that was clear now. She'd asked Declan to do something he clearly couldn't do. She couldn't even convince herself that he just wasn't ready yet; she was afraid he never would be. She didn't blame him, after the horror of his life, it was a wonder he functioned at all, but still. . .

She missed him already, she thought as she stood up. Missed him, the slow smiles that had begun to come more often, the quirky humor, the laughs even more precious because of their rarity, the way he looked at her when they were just talking, as if what she was saying was the only thing that mattered.

The way he looked at her when he was about to kiss her. The way he looked at her after he had. The way he looked at her as he undressed her, touched her, slid himself inside her. . .

She let out a low moan as need nearly cramped her body double. What had she done? She should have just dealt with things as they were, not tried to fix him. Why did she always have to try and fix things? She rescued horses, not people, she should have just let him be—

The view through the side window of the trailer finally registered.

Flames. Heading down the rise. Toward her. And the horses.

Everything else was jolted out of her head. She ran then, stopping for nothing, because nothing she had was more important than keeping the horses safe. She thought swiftly as she leapt to the ground, forgoing the steps. She couldn't assume it wouldn't get here . . . she had to assume it would. For their sake. She tried to judge how fast it was moving. Did she have time to halter them and build a string? She could ride Granite . . . he'd be steady enough once she had a bridle on him.

She reached the corral, saw they were nervous already. Even she could smell the smoke, so it had to be stingingly obvious to the horse's much more powerful sense of smell. As she got closer, she could feel their edginess, how strong it was, and guessed one more close strike might set them off. But the herd instinct was strong, and they might follow her and Granite.

She left the gate closed but unlatched. Last resort, she thought as she ran to the small shed and grabbed Granite's bridle and an armful of halters, she would just have to turn them loose to escape the fire, and trust she could find them all later.

Granite wasn't happy, tossing his head as she tried to bridle him. Her own nerves were probably just adding to the problem; from this angle she could see the flames were moving fast, faster than she'd hoped. They'd be at the corner of the big corral in minutes, if that. She saw another flash of light, but this one oddly seemed to come from the ground up. She couldn't take time to look.

"Come on, baby, now's not the time, that's it, easy now," she crooned, and the big gray finally took the bit.

She left him ground tied, hoping his training would hold even in the face of this, and started toward the others. They were genuinely spooked now, and she realized she wasn't going to be able to halter them all in time. She—

Something moved at the edge of her vision, outside the corral. Someone? Something trying to escape as well? Then Oliver let out a snorting neigh. And the shadow resolved into a human shape.

Declan.

He ran to her. "Are you all right?"

"Fine. I've got to get them out of here, the fire—"

"My place. I turned the water system on, so everything will be wet. And the barn's got fire sprinklers. I called it in on the way here."

She realized that despite how they'd parted, he'd come with a complete understanding and acceptance of her priority, and prepared to help her accomplish it. She wanted to hug him, but there was no time.

"Rope," he said, looking around. "Or a lunge line should do it."

Quickly, she sorted it out of the pile of gear she'd grabbed. The smoke was getting thicker, and she didn't know how long they'd have before the horses truly panicked. He took it and ran, clearing the top rail of the corral in a rather elegant hand assisted leap. She turned back to trying to get the rest of the horses haltered, trusting he knew what he was doing. In less than a minute he was back. He dug into the pile and brought out a halter with a lead line attached.

"I'll get Oliver. Don't mess with the rest. They should follow us, if we ride through the gate."

She looked where he'd gestured as he went for the horse that had actually started toward him. She saw that he'd tied the lunge line from the corral fence to the back of his Jeep, parked back near the gate they'd used so often. The light she'd seen, she realized, had been the headlights as he came over the rise. And now, he'd created a makeshift chute, to channel the horses onto his land.

It would work. She was sure it would work. It had to work, because the flames were licking at the corral now, and the dry wood would go up easily. But once they got through the gate they'd be far enough from the flames and the herd would stick together as he'd said.

And then he was there, mounted bareback on Oliver. He'd rigged the lead line into makeshift reins fastened on the halter. She grabbed a hunk of mane at Granite's withers and swung aboard.

And there, in the midst of thunder, lightning, and fire, they led their little band to safety.

THE HORSES SETTLED almost immediately once they were gathered in his barn, out of sight of the flames, although Kelsey was sure they could still smell the smoke. She slid off Granite, realizing as she hit the ground and her knees nearly gave way, that she was shaking. The aftermath of the adrenaline rush, she guessed. Before she could pull herself together Declan was there. He practically yanked her into his arms, hugging her fiercely.

"Thank you," she whispered against his chest.

And as if her simple words had broken a dam words flooded from him.

"God, Kels, I was so scared for you. I was already going to come to you, when it started. And I knew you'd never leave them, you'd kill yourself trying to save them. I couldn't let it end that way, like that, not us. I'm a mess, I know that, but I've never cared, I just got by and that was all that mattered. But now. . . you matter more than anything ever has to me, please, Kels, I'll try, I swear I'll try, whatever you want."

Kelsey understood the magnitude of those last words. She slipped her arms around him, tightened them.

"I'll ask you to say that again, when things are calmer."

"I'll say it again now." He loosened his embrace, looked down at her. "I'll say it as often as you want, and I'll do it. I didn't think I was even capable of feeling like this. And it took me too damned long to realize what it is. I've never been here before, so I didn't know. Until I saw those flames headed for you and I realized that if I lost you, I'd lose everything."

"Deck—"

"We'll set up your horse camp, and I'll be there. If you think I can help kids like me, I'll be there. I know I'm not going to be very good at it at first, but I won't quit. I swear to you I won't."

"Deck—"

"That barbecue? I'll go. You want to parade through the town square? I'll do it. You want me to put up a sign, take out an ad, get a tattoo, I'll do it."

She couldn't help smiling at that last one.

"And what would that tattoo say?"

He reached up to cup her face. "It would say 'Worth Any Risk.'"

Her breath caught at that, but she lost it altogether at his next words.

"I love you, Kelsey Blaine."

A warmth, wider and deeper than anything any fire could bring, billowed through her in a rush. "And I love you, Crazy Joseph Declan Kilcoyne Bolt. In all your incarnations."

It wasn't until much later that they realized the cavalry had arrived, and that half of Whiskey River had turned out to fight the lightning sparked wildfire. They secured the barn and started down the rise, seeing from here that while most of the corral was gone, and the shed scorched, her trailer and the rest had been saved. She saw Trey Kelly's truck pulled in alongside his half brother, Xander Blue's. And further on, she saw the Banner's delivery truck, and amazingly even old Henry "Doc" Teller, all eighty-five years of him, apparently directing people.

She felt Declan pause beside her at the sight of so many of the townspeople, all gathered to help one of their own. She stayed quiet. This wasn't going to be easy for him, and it had to be his decision. She heard him take in a deep breath, and she reached out and took his hand. His fingers tightened around hers. She squeezed back, sending him what strength she could. He swallowed audibly.

"Let's go thank them," he said.

And in that moment, she knew he'd truly meant everything he'd said.

Chapter Twenty-Nine

DECLAN BRACED HIMSELF. He'd agreed to this, even encouraged it, but every nerve he had was curling up in fear, screaming at him to run.

He would not run.

He had promised Kelsey he would see this through. He had yet to break any of the promises he'd made to her, and he never would. She reached out, grabbed his hand, squeezed it. He took from it the strength she always gave him.

"I love you," he said. It came easily now, and grew more true every day.

"And I love you," Kelsey said.

And then she reached up to knock on the cheerful blue door.

Declan sucked in a deep, harsh breath as the door to the small, tidy beach house swung open. A woman stood there, looking younger than the fifty he knew she was, tall, elegant, and with Kelsey's eyes. Kelsey's brilliant, blue eyes. For a moment he couldn't think, and if she spoke he missed it as Kelsey urged him inside. She turned to close the door behind them, leaving him to face the woman alone for a moment. And he had the feeling he was seeing his future, what Kelsey would look like in twenty years or so. And he finally found words to speak.

"So. It runs in the family."

Lisa Blaine smiled. "The eyes? Yes, we do share those."

"I meant the beauty," Declan said.

She laughed then. "Oh, she gets more of that from her father. But I thank you anyway."

"And the brains?" he asked.

"That I'll take some credit for," she said. "My girl is clever, quick, kind, generous, and altogether amazing."

He'd never heard a voice with such honest pride in another. He realized with a little shock of pleasure he felt no bitterness that Kelsey had had what he never did, a mother like this. He was simply glad, because this woman had raised the daughter who had broken through, and dragged him back into the world. The daughter who, after the first few moments, had left them to work out who they would be to each other.

"With questionable taste in men," he said wryly. "For which I'm very glad."

Lisa Blaine studied him for a long moment. Then she said softly, "You are, aren't you." It wasn't a question, but an acknowledgment.

"Yes."

She smiled, nodded. "Kelsey knows what she wants, and

she's not afraid to go after it. I raised her that way. But she also has a reservoir of compassion and caring so deep I have yet to find the bottom of it."

"Too much, sometimes."

"Perhaps. But I think you've needed it."

He couldn't deny it, wouldn't, because it would be a lie and he wouldn't lie to this woman. "Yes."

"But you also have something she's never given anyone else."

For a moment, all he could think of was last night, the hours spent in his bed, indulging the hunger that only grew with every encounter, a wild, crazy night that he knew he would never forget.

"That, too," Lisa said with a wry smile that succeeded in making him flush with embarrassment that Kelsey's mother had read him so clearly. "But she's given you her heart, Declan. Don't break it."

"I—"

"One more thing."

He stopped, feeling as if he'd been called before a judge and jury, and certain he was going to be found guilty before he'd even said another word.

"Kelsey's a package deal," she said. His brow furrowed. "I come with her. Oh, I don't mean I'll intrude on your lives or always be around, but I will be there. I'm always there if my girl needs me."

"I know."

And he did. It had been a fascinating sort of torture, seeing how close Kelsey and her mother were. At first he'd tried to tell himself it was a female thing, but he knew it would have been the same had Kelsey been a boy. And glad as he was for her, his mind still tried to grapple with thoughts of what it must have been like, to grow up with a mother like that.

"And now," Lisa went on watching him intently, "you're part of that package. My daughter loves you so I love you, for that alone, but I feel certain it will soon be for your own sake. And so I will always be there for you, too, if you need me."

Declan stared at her. He heard her words, but the foreign concept was too much for him to wrap his mind around quickly. What he knew intellectually, that most parents loved their children, had never made it to his heart, his gut, because he'd never known it firsthand.

"I know it will take time for you to trust that, and that's fine. I'm patient."

He couldn't speak. He who made his living with words had none for this.

"Will you let me, Declan?" Lisa asked, reaching out to lay a gently hand on his arm. "Will you let me be there for you? Give you support when you need it, help when you want it, and love all the time? Will you let me be the mother you never had?"

His throat was so tight it was almost impossible to even

breathe. He had to look away, but the image of her eyes, Kelsey's eyes, so warm and giving, was so vivid it was as if he were still staring at her. He swallowed, or tried to past the knot in his throat. She didn't move, didn't turn away, she stayed there in the silence, with the same sort of gentle determination her daughter had.

"Promise me." He barely managed to get it out, still unable to meet her gaze.

"Promise you what?"

"That. . . you'll tell me. If I. . . hurt her without realizing." He swallowed again. Stared at the ground. Found the rest of the words. "You know her like no one does. If I start down a wrong path with her. . . if I let. . . the past get too important. . ."

"I'll rein you in like one of her horses," Lisa promised.

He looked at her than. He didn't know what to say to this woman who had given him two wondrous gifts, the woman he loved and a place in her own heart.

So he hugged her instead. Tight.

She hugged him back. Tight.

It was enough.

And when Kelsey came back to check on them, he thought the look on her face as she saw them was the most beautiful thing he'd ever seen.

KELSEY COULD HEAR the chatter. It all made her smile. But she'd been doing a lot of that in the last six months.

"I have never seen a crowd like this in Whiskey River, not even at Boots and Bangles."

"Every kid in the county must be here."

"Not just the county, they're from everywhere, all over the country and even the world. See the family over there, with the three boys? They flew in from Australia."

"He's really never done this before?"

"Never. Aren't the costumes great?"

The line had wrapped around the entire square, younger children with their parents in tow, older ones clustered in groups, talking excitedly. The enthusiasm had built to a fever pitch in the weeks since the news had been announced, that on release day Declan Bolt would do his first ever public appearance. A book-signing of the new Sam Smith adventure at Whiskey River Books. The publisher had crashed their schedule to get the book out at Christmas, and it was paying off handsomely.

"He's going to bring as much business to Whiskey River in a day as we bring in in a year," Trey Kelly said with a grin.

His brother nodded. "I'll pass on the chocolate covered crickets, though."

"Me, too. But let's not forget our own miracle worker, who lured him out to do this," Juliette said, nodding toward where Kelsey stood watching her fiancé sign yet another of the huge stack of books on the table beside him. There were unopened cartons behind him, but Mel was still worried there wouldn't be enough; the turnout had dwarfed even her lofty expectations.

"Pretty sweet dedication," Megan said to Kelsey, holding up the copy of the book she'd bought, planning on reading it to her niece.

They all laughed as Kelsey blushed. But she was smiling as she turned back to listening to each person in the long line. Some simply said that they loved the books, many were kids said they had hated reading until Sam had come along, most had questions about what this or that really meant, and was this character really what they seemed. And every once in a while a story would come pouring out that made her eyes sting, a kid saying the books had given him hope, helped her hang on, given him the courage to escape. She watched Declan in those moments, saw the stories healing him, and smiled wider through the threatening tears.

She'd cried more than once since he'd finished this book. She'd read it in manuscript form, and while Sam's tribulations and the way he'd met them had, as always, amazed and inspired, she had broken down when the character she'd expected, the police officer who would be Sam's eventual salvation, entered the story. For the cop was a woman, and her name was Lisa.

She picked up one of the books, ran her fingers over the cover, tracing the lettering of his name. She opened it, found her way to the dedication page. Not that she needed to look.

The words had been etched into her mind from the moment he had handed her that page to read last. She'd barely been able to see the page through the tears that had begun anew at the end of the story.

To Kelsey Blaine, who rescues a lot more than horses and has the biggest heart in all of Texas. I love you. Marry me?

The moments that followed would be a treasure she would hold in her mind and heart forever. And she knew then that Sam—and the man she loved—would triumph. She even thought, after watching him with the kids at the horse camp, that maybe someday, when he was certain he wouldn't pass along his grim heritage, he would think about a child of their own. But if not, that was fine too; there were plenty of kids who needed Declan Bolt's—and Sam Smith's—brand of understanding and help.

And she, she thought now with an inward smile, would become of all things, Kelsey Kilcoyne.

Much later, long after the midnight signing was done, the children had been carted home by parents muttering that it was a good thing it was a weekend because their offspring were obviously going to be up all night reading, she and Declan took a sunrise ride, she on Granite and he on the now sleek and healthy—and much loved—Oliver.

They passed the burned spot, where half of Whiskey River had turned out to fight the blaze together, the night that had been the turning point for many things. They both looked at it, and where it had been stopped short of the shed and the hay shelter. Then at each other, and she knew he was thinking of the same thing she was, that moment when, horses safe, he'd grabbed her told her everything she'd ever wanted to hear from him.

On a low rise overlooking the river they halted, and dismounted to watch the huge orange sun begin to burst over the horizon.

"Fitting, since you came into my life," he said as he reached out and took her hand.

"What?"

"Riding like this. Not into the sunset, but the sunrise. Because that's how I feel. It's finally morning."

He did have a way with words. . .

And she kissed him.

The End

Love the town of Whiskey River, Texas? Stay awhile. Where the women are feisty, the men are sexy and the romance is hotter than ever.

The Brothers of Whiskey River Series

If you enjoyed **Whiskey River Rescue**, you'll love the other Whiskey River stories!

Book 1: **Texas Heirs** by Eve Gaddy and Katherine Garbera

Book 2: **Texas Cowboy** by Eve Gaddy

Book 3: **Texas Tycoon** by Katherine Garbera

Book 4: **Texas Rebel** by Eve Gaddy

Book 5: **Texas Lover** by Katherine Garbera

Book 6: **Texas Bachelor** by Eve Gaddy and Katherine Garbera

Available now at your favorite online retailer!

About the Author

Author of more than 70 books, (she sold her first ten in less than two years) Justine Davis is a five time winner of the coveted RWA RITA Award, including for being inducted into the RWA Hall of Fame. A fifteen time nominee for RT Book Review awards, she has won four times, received three of their lifetime achievement awards, and had four titles on the magazine's 200 Best of all Time list. Her books have appeared on national best seller lists, including USA Today. She has been featured on CNN, taught at several national and international conferences, and at the UCLA writer's program.

After years of working in law enforcement, and more years doing both, Justine now writes full time. She lives near beautiful Puget Sound in Washington State, peacefully coexisting with deer, bears, a pair of bald eagles, a tailless raccoon, and her beloved '67 Corvette roadster. When she's not writing, taking photographs, or driving said roadster (and yes, it goes very fast) she tends to her knitting. Literally.

Visit Justine at her website at JustineDavis.com

Thank you for reading

Whiskey River Rescue

If you enjoyed this book, you can find more from all our great authors at TulePublishing.com, or from your favorite online retailer.

TULE
PUBLISHING

92731475R10164

Made in the USA
Lexington, KY
08 July 2018